TWELVE DAYS

A JOHN MILTON THRILLER

MARK DAWSON

PART I

THE TWELFTH DAY

1

Pinky stood outside the door to the house, amped up, ready to do what they had come here to do. There were four of them: Chips was on the other side of the door, a large firework in one hand and a lighter in the other; Kidz was next to Pinky, letting his baseball bat swing to and fro in a loose double-handed grip; Little Mark was next to Kidz, big enough that he didn't need a weapon.

"Ready?" Pinky asked them.

They nodded. They'd done this before. They were buzzing with anticipation, but none of them were scared. The property was a 'cuckoo' house, owned by a man who had slipped out of the reach of social services and who liked a smoke. All the local gangs looked for people like him: easily manipulated by offers of friendship or free gear and then, when their guard was down, exploited for all that they were worth. Remedials or accommodating addicts, it didn't matter; anyone with a house that the gang could invade and take over was fair game.

This man's name was Neal. The social had given him a one-bedroom flat in a low-rise in Stoke Newington. Pinky had been inside before and knew the layout: kitchen, living room, bathroom, bedroom. The last time he had been inside, there had been a group of crackheads smoking on the sofa in the living room and a couple of junkies shooting up in the bedroom. They had watched the flat for a couple of hours today, and they expected to find a similar clientele. More to the point, Lucky was inside, and Pinky had business with him.

"Let's do it."

They were each wearing the purple bandana that marked them out as London Fields Boys. Pinky still felt pride when he thought of the gang, what it represented and how he had risen through it in the last three years. He had been a shotter—a low-level drug dealer—and a thief when he had started out, but he was more than that now. He was an elder: nineteen years old and influential, with a reputation to match. He'd built that rep by doing things like this. Today would remind everyone that he was a player, someone serious, someone you didn't want to mess around with.

Pinky pulled the bandana up so that it covered his nose and mouth, pulled his hood forward so that it rested behind the brim of his Raiders cap, and stepped aside so that Little Mark could face the door.

Pinky reached into his pocket for his piece. It was a Glock 17; he'd stolen it off a dealer who had been foolish enough to try selling his shit in the ends that belonged to the LFB. Pinky had followed him back to his car and knifed him as he was getting inside. He had done it to send a message—Sol had ordered it, and Pinky had been happy to comply—but as he frisked the guy and searched his car, he found five grand and the gun in the glovebox. The cherry on top of the cake.

Pinky turned to Chips and nodded. He had the Catherine wheel in his hand; Pinky had bought ten of them from an online store just before Bonfire Night and had kept them for occasions like this. He had played a lot of *Call of Duty* and watched a lot of YouTube videos of soldiers busting into buildings, and he knew how important it was to disorient anyone you wanted to get the jump on. He'd used fireworks before. They worked perfectly.

Chips thumbed the lighter and lit the firework, both fuses hissing as the flames trailed up towards the gunpowder. Little Mark took a step back, breathed in, raised his foot and stomped it against the door, aiming for the spot just below the handle. The place wasn't secure, with no metal grille or entryphone, and the door was just the same thin plywood replacement that had been put in place after the police had used a battering ram to break down the last one. It flew open, bounced off the wall and crashed back into the frame. Little Mark stood aside to give Chips the chance to do his thing.

The door to the living room was open, and Chips's aim was good. The firework bounced once, then twice, skittering through the door and rolling to a stop inside the room. There was a beat and then it caught light, spewing out multicoloured sparks in all directions as it started to spin.

"Now!" Pinky yelled, his voice muffled by the bandana.

2

They went in: Pinky first, then Kidz, then Little Mark, then Chips. Kidz and Little Mark went into the bedroom, and Pinky and Chips waited at the doorway to the living room. The firework was still spinning, spraying its sparks into all four corners of the room and sending out disorientating whizzes and pops. There were five customers inside, three on an old settee and the other two on the floor. They had been smoking crack, although the distinctive smell of the drug had been overwhelmed by the smell of the gunpowder as the firework completed its revolutions and fizzled out.

Pinky raised the gun and went inside.

Lucky was on the settee, and, as he saw Pinky come inside, he tried to scurry away. There was nowhere for him to go; Pinky reached him and pressed the muzzle of the gun right up against his forehead. Pinky felt the adrenaline, the prickle of excitement that ran up and down his spine, and drank it all in. The sound of Little Mark and Kidz clearing out the bedroom faded as Pinky pressed the gun harder, pushing Lucky back into the cushions of the settee.

Lucky, Pinky thought, sneering. *What a joke. You ain't so lucky now.*

"Please," Lucky begged.

"You fucked me over," Pinky said. "Fucked us all over. What did you think was gonna happen? You think I'd just lie down and take it like I'm your bitch? You don't know me that well. You don't know me at all, blood."

"I swear I didn't know they was there, man." Lucky's eyes moistened as he started to cry. "I would never do that."

"You wouldn't?"

"No, man. *Never*. I ain't mad, am I? I swear."

He was called Lucky on account of the fact that he had been pulled by the police with half a key in the back of his car and they had let him go without finding it. He was five years older than Pinky, but he had always deferred to the younger man. Pinky was nineteen, tall and skinny and with acne scars across his face. He had an angular face, with a hook nose and pointed cheekbones that seemed to stretch out his skin. His eyes were flat and deadened, rarely showing emotion. Pinky knew that the others spoke about that, about how his eyes never showed humanity. He knew that they were scared of him, and he made sure it stayed that way. Fear had brought Pinky to the top, and it would keep him there.

"Please," Lucky begged again. "You ain't got to do this. I know I fucked up. Let me fix it."

Pinky leaned forward, pressing harder on the gun. His mouth was right next to Lucky's ear. "You know what happens when you cross me, right? When you cross the LFB?"

There was history in that name. Meaning. Pinky remembered the young man who used to run the LFB: Pops. He had forgotten that and Pinky had dooked him. Murdered him, cold-blooded, ruthless. Bizness had forgotten it, too, got himself distracted so that the old white guy could take him out that same night as the riots that had torn up the East End. That night might have spelled the end of it all, but Pinky hadn't been ready to call it quits. He had taken a bag of cocaine and cash from Bizness's studio and started his own little business. He had done well and had attracted the attention of Bizness's brother. Solomon Brown had got back in the game and made Pinky his lieutenant. It worked, most of the time.

"Who was it, Lucky? Who took my gear?"

He held the gun steady. All Pinky would need to do was put a little extra pressure on the trigger and Lucky would be gone. This was it, what he lived for, the power over life and death.

"They jumped me. I didn't see their faces. They said they were going to kill me unless I told them where the gear was. What was I supposed to do, man?"

Pinky leaned in close, saw Lucky's dark skin glistening under the light bulb hanging above them, watched a bead of sweat as it rolled down from his scalp and slid down his cheek. Lucky scrunched up his face and began to shake. The smell of piss wafted up through the crack and the gunpowder.

"Boy gone and pissed himself!" Chips said, drawing nervous laughter from the other addicts.

The others knew what would be coming next. They had seen it before. There had to be consequences. Someone crossed you, they had to pay. That was how it was. Pinky didn't know whether Lucky had been stupid or whether he had betrayed him. It didn't matter. He couldn't let it go. The others stared, eyes wide. Doing nothing wasn't one of the options. He needed to keep his reputation as someone you didn't cross. Lucky started crying and begging for his life, but it didn't make a difference. This was how things were. You were nothing without your rep. It was the law of the jungle. You let yourself get weak and someone would try to take advantage.

"I'm gonna count to three," Pinky said. "One. Two..."

"It was Bones and Digger," Lucky whined. "They said they were moving into the neighbourhood, that they were going to take the ends around Blissett House, that I either sold them the gear or they'd kill me and take it. They said they knew where I lived, where my family lives, Tanesha... I didn't have a choice, man."

That was all he needed to know. Bones and Digger, part of the Stokey crew, the gang who had started to nibble at the territory that belonged to the LFB. There was a drill MC, Shetty, who had started posting videos on YouTube saying what Stokey was going to do to the LFB. Chips had gone up to Stoke Newington High Street in the summer, and someone had spotted him; he had been stabbed in the bagel shop, almost bleeding to death before the ambulance got to him. The videos had started with Shetty saying that Chips was the first, that they were all going to get done.

And now this.

Fuck this.

Pinky took the gun away, placing it on Lucky's knee. "Well done," he said. "But you still got to pay."

"Pinky!"

Pinky turned. Kidz was standing in the doorway.

"What?"

"Shit, man. Sorry... I didn't know..."

Pinky loosened his grip on Lucky, allowing him to crumple back against the settee. "What is it?"

"The TV in the other room... You won't believe it."

Pinky told Chips to keep an eye on Lucky and followed Kidz into the bedroom. It was a mess: the bed was unmade, a stained mattress visible beneath crumpled sheets. Two addicts were on the floor, leaning against the wall, out of their minds on junk. Sky Sports was on. Pinky watched as a black man appeared on the screen and began to talk. Pinky's eyes narrowed and his nostrils flared with anger. The man's hands were wrapped in white tape, and there was a boxing ring behind him. The name on the screen said Mustafa Muhammad, but that wasn't his real name. Pinky knew him. They all did. He was bigger than when he was last in these ends, taller now and full of muscle, but it was the same little bitch Pinky remembered.

Elijah.

Pinky listened.

"I'm just working hard, concentrating on my next fight. Connolly's good, a tough fighter, but he's never stepped into the ring with someone like me. I'm gonna knock him out, and then we can talk about who's next."

The others listened expectantly, waiting for Pinky to react.

"Look at baby JaJa," he said. "All growed up."

"Where the fuck's he been hiding?" Little Mark said.

"Changed his name and everything," Chips said.

Pinky had looked into what had happened to JaJa. He and his mum had disappeared a month after their flat had been torched and Bizness had been shot. JaJa had betrayed Pinky to the police, and he had ghosted before Pinky could show him what a stupid thing that had been to do. Three years ago, Pinky thought, casting his mind back. Seemed like JaJa had been busy in the meantime.

Pinky found the remote on the bed, wound the footage back, and played it again. JaJa was bigger, with muscle on his shoulders and arms and neatly defined abs that glistened with sweat. Pinky had pushed him around before, but he had stayed thin and slender while JaJa had filled out; it wouldn't be as easy to push him around today.

"I googled him," Kidz said. He looked down at his phone and read: "'As an amateur, Mustafa Muhammad fought for Sheffield City Boxing Club, winning nineteen fights out of twenty. He scored a first-round stoppage over Ben Arnfield in his first professional fight and then won his next seven fights after that, winning by knockout in all of them.'"

Sheffield, Pinky thought. *So that's where he went.*

Kidz summarised the rest of the article he had found: "His next fight is in London. They're saying if he wins, he'll be fighting for a belt next year. They say he's going to make mad money."

Pinky sneered before breaking into a toothy grin. "Little JaJa's on his way to the big time. Time we said hello to him again."

PART II

THE ELEVENTH DAY

3

The air that drifted in from the sea was warm and almost cloying. There was no wind, but the stillness suited him. Even though it was evening, the temperature was still warm enough that John Milton could sit in shorts and a T-shirt without worrying about shivering in the cold. He sat at the bar waiting for the barman to finish mixing his second virgin cocktail and, as was his habit, glanced around to see who else was here with him. There were a few other people out tonight, but otherwise it was quiet. That was why Milton had chosen the town of Arafo; cheap flights and a consistent climate had made Tenerife popular with tourists all year round, but this was off the beaten track. It would have been busier in Santa Cruz or Puerto de la Cruz, or any of the coastal hotspots that drew in the package tourists, but Milton had selected carefully to avoid them. He was here to surf, to go hiking in the interior, and to enjoy the Christmas season in a pleasant climate.

He had been in Brazil until recently, although his trip to the Rock in Rio festival hadn't been the relaxing experience that he had expected. He had found himself involved with one of the gangsters who ran the underworld in the *favelas*, and been forced to respond to the betrayal of an old friend. That was all done now, but Milton had left the country still in need of the relaxation that he had travelled there to find. Arafo had delivered.

The barman placed the drink in front of him, then turned back to the television screen that had been placed on the opposite end of the bar. Milton picked up the drink, removing the umbrella and the fruit before taking a sip and placing it back down. He glanced at the screen. A piece of tinsel had been draped across it in honour of the time of year, the same colour as the decorations on the small artificial tree that had been placed behind the bar. Madrid and Barcelona had fought out a two-two draw earlier, but now the *Classico* had given way to boxing. A caption on the screen identified the fight as Muhammad v Cantrell and indicated that it was a replay from two months earlier.

Milton watched the bout. A muscular black fighter was schooling his smaller white opponent. He kept him on the end of a long jab, firing it out with metronomic regularity, before softening his body with a nasty right hook into the kidneys. The black man stepped out of range as his opponent tried to counter. The camera zoomed in on the face of the white guy: he was blowing hard, and his cheeks and eyebrows were already reddened. Another caption appeared on the screen: it was still the first round.

The barman noticed that Milton was watching. "*Él es bueno.*"

Milton's Spanish was average at best, but he nodded his agreement. "He's very good."

The barman ducked and moved with the boxer's movements. Another counter was slipped, a left jab coming from the black fighter before he swung down to the side and detonated an unorthodox, unexpected and utterly devastating right hook on his opponent's chin.

There was a gasp from the other patrons of the bar as the punch landed.

"*Increíble!*" the barman exclaimed.

The white guy was out before he hit the canvas. The referee stood over him, waving off the count, cradling the boxer's head and removing his mouthguard. The winner stood on the ropes and saluted the crowd.

The camera zoomed on his face. Milton's eyes narrowed. He had a moment of recognition, swiftly replaced by confusion.

"*¡Coño, chico!*" the barman swore. Milton raised his glass in reply and nodded his head. The knockout was impressive, but he was still confused.

The shot changed to a wide angle of the ring. Medical staff gathered around the prone fighter, who was only now showing signs of consciousness. The MC stepped through the ropes and made his way to the centre of the ring, where the victor was waiting.

"*Volumen?*" Milton asked, twisting his fingers to indicate that he wanted to listen to what was being said.

The barman reached under the bar for a remote control.

"Ladies and gentlemen, referee Tony Gaitskill stops the fight at one minute forty-five seconds into the first round. The winner, by technical knockout—the Sheffield Express, Mustafa 'Boom Boom' Muhammad."

Milton stared at the screen, a smile on his face.

The victor moved to the ring apron and sat down. An interviewer, hidden behind the camera, held a microphone in front of the man's face.

"Mustafa," he said, *"that was very impressive."*

"Thank you. I knew I had to get him out of there early. Wanted to make a statement."

"You certainly did that," the interviewer said. *"That's nine fights, nine wins, and all of them by knockout. What's next?"*

"We move on. Everyone knows what fight I want."

"Let's bring your promoter in now." A man in a suit shuffled into the shot, sitting down next to his sweaty protégé. *"That was some display."*

The boxer was on his feet and, as the cameraman was jostled backwards by a swell in the crowd around the ring, Milton got a better look at him: taller, more muscular, his black skin offset by the deep gold of his shorts.

He might have changed his name, but Milton knew exactly who he was.

Elijah Warriner.

A caption on the screen identified the promoter as Tommy Porter. *"First off,"* Porter said, *"I just want to say a big thank you to all those who came out to York Hall tonight for a great night of boxing. The fans make this place special, and tonight was no different. But even the best things come to an end, and I don't think Mustafa will be fighting in somewhere as small as this again. He's destined for the top, and he only wants the big fights. I mean, come on—this kid just turned nineteen and he's been knocking out everyone we've put in front of him. Nine fights, nine KOs. He needs to move on, probably quicker than any of us ever expected, but that doesn't matter. He's a special talent, and people might think we're rushing him, but you can't wait around with someone like this. He's ready."*

"So who's next?"

"It's the one everyone wants to see. I can announce it now: Christmas Eve at the Copper Box, London, Mustafa Muhammad versus Samuel Connolly. A Christmas cracker for fight fans."

Milton raised his eyebrows as the crowd cheered behind

the men on screen. He didn't follow the sport as much as he would have liked, but even he was surprised at the step-up. York Hall held a thousand people at best. The Copper Box was on the Olympic Park and must have held six or seven thousand.

The interviewer reached out for Elijah's elbow and brought him back into shot. *"Finally, Mustafa, we've been reading this week about how you've dedicated this to your mum."*

"Yeah, you know I do all this for my family so they can have a better life. My mum's the reason I'm where I am today. She's had to deal with the worst of it, but she's a fighter. No one can keep her down."

Milton remembered Sharon. Elijah's mother had led a difficult life, and then she had been caught up in the aftermath of his clumsy attempt to wrest her son from the orbit of the man who had threatened to blight his future. It had been more than three years since then. Milton had thought of her often, and about the way he had left without speaking to her or her boy. He had never been happy with it, but there had been nothing else that he could have done. Control had sent a psychopath to kill him, and an innocent man had been murdered in the crossfire. Milton had been shot, too, and had had no choice but to flee. He had reflected on it since, many times, and had never been able to shake the feeling that he had left unfinished business behind him that evening.

Milton watched as Elijah smiled, and he couldn't help but smile back.

Maybe he could draw a line through it. Enough time had passed. He could go to London now; Control's death had made that possible. He had been living there, working in the cabman's shelter in Russell Square. He kept a low profile, but there was no need to hide. They weren't looking for him any longer.

There was no reason to wait: he would go back to visit the young man he'd once known.

And saved.

PART III

THE TENTH DAY

4

Pinky sat with his back against the brick structure on the roof of Blissett House. He loved coming up here. The block was twenty-two storeys tall, seventy metres high, and the view was spectacular: he could see the grid of untidy streets that made up this part of Hackney, the main roads that fed the city, the open space of Victoria Park and, not that far away, the illuminated London Stadium that had hosted the Olympics. Pinky had been coming up here for years, ever since he had taught himself how to pick the padlock on the access door. He had kept the secret to himself. It was his special place, somewhere only he knew about, a place to come when he wanted a moment's peace, somewhere he could try to silence the voices in his head.

Pinky's real name was Shaquille, although only his mum still called him that. He didn't even think of himself that way anymore. They had called him Pinky ever since he was little. His old man had bought him a knock-off Tampa Bay Buccaneers jersey that he had been wanting for months, but when his mum put it into the washing machine for the first time, all the colour had run out of it so that it was more fuchsia than red. He'd wanted to throw it in the rubbish, but his dad had threatened him with a beating for being ungrateful and had made him wear it. The other kids on the block thought it was hilarious, said wearing it meant he must be gay, and that was that; they'd called him Pinky and the name had stuck.

He had hated it at first, but he didn't care now. No one would dare to insult him. He'd worked hard to build his reputation, and everyone on the estate knew that to wind him up was a risk not worth taking. They all knew he had blood on his hands. Pops had been his first—four shots into his body as they walked through Victoria Park near the Old Ford Road. There had been others since: a little thief from E7 Crips who had been rolling commuters on the East London line; a dealer from Bethnal Green Massive who thought he could sell his smack to the addicts who usually bought from Pinky's crew. There had been other demonstrations of his ruthlessness—he was known for his blades, swiping them across the cheeks of those he wanted to bear witness to his mercilessness—and it had all contributed to his rep.

Pinky had taken over the LFB in the aftermath of the week that saw Pops's death and then the murder of Risky Bizness, everything spiralling into the abyss as riots swept out of Tottenham and consumed the capital during that long, hot summer. That was three years ago; he had just been a younger then, but now he was a Face. He was Sol's man in Hackney. He ran these ends.

He stood up, his jeans hanging down loose. He felt the heavy weight of his gold chain as it fell back against his chest, and ran his fingers over the chunky links. It had cost him a grand, and he had another one hidden under his bed at home. He put up his hood, patted the bulge of the butterfly knife in his pocket, and made his way to the door that led to the stairs. He had an appointment to keep, and the man he was seeing was not someone you wanted to keep waiting.

5

Pinky turned down the volume on the fifty-inch widescreen television on the wall—silencing the boxer on the screen talking—then turned to the man sitting next to him.

"There," he said. "I told you."

Solomon Brown took a drag on the joint he was holding, then blew the smoke in Pinky's face. Pinky felt his eyes watering, but swallowed back the cough that tickled his throat. The man was almost a foot taller than Pinky, and there was muscle there, too, straining against the fabric of the black T-shirt the man was wearing.

"You sure?" Brown said, looking at the glowing end of the joint, then blowing softly on it to make it glow a little brighter.

"It's him, Sol," Pinky said. "I grew up with him."

Brown took another drag and then offered the joint to Pinky.

"So, what you saying? He's been in Sheffield?"

"That's what they say," Pinky replied, taking the joint and sucking hard on it. The weed was smoother than the crap they were pushing on the street now. The cats all wanted skunk these days, weed from unpollinated plants that had more THC than hash or grass. Pinky preferred a smoother smoke and was glad that Sol felt the same way.

"You did well. Bringing this to me."

Pinky relaxed a little. Sol had always freaked him out. He'd spent enough time in his presence to know he had it in him to lose his rag. There wasn't that much difference between him and his brother in that regard: both of them could go from easy-going to mental at the drop of a hat. Sol contrasted in other ways: he was smart, he had been to college, and he ran the business like it was a company, with accounts and ledgers and a structure that had never been there when Bizness had been in charge. Sol made no secret of the fact that he was smart, and the fact that he wasn't ashamed of that made his angry outbursts more unsettling.

There had been a vacuum in the aftermath of his brother's death, and Sol had filled it. He had steadied the ship and then retrenched their position. Pinky knew of six rivals who had ended up shanked or shot in the week that followed. He had shot one of them himself. Sol had wiped out anyone who might have thought that they could muscle into the borough; he'd eliminated his rivals and laid down an example to everyone else who thought that Bizness's murder might have signalled a changing of the guard. It didn't.

Pinky gestured to the screen. "We can't let it slide. After what JaJa did? He needs to pay. Can't have someone like him making a name for himself without paying his dues."

"Hush your mouth," Brown said, snatching the joint back, then crumpling the last third of it into a saucer that was being used for an ashtray. "You think I don't know that? My blood is dead because of him. He owes me. He's the reason I'm the only one left. He's the reason I ain't got no brother no more."

They watched as Elijah lifted himself from the ring apron and walked into the crowd and towards the dressing room.

"So he's good?" Sol asked.

"He's good. They say if he wins the next fight, he'll be fighting for a belt."

"Boy does that, he's looking at mad money."

"Millions," Pinky agreed.

Sol paused the screen with Elijah looking into the camera. "And look at him: pretty boy, come up from the streets, done good for himself; looks after his mum, built himself a life. He's going to be marketable. Nike and Adidas—man, they'll be throwing money at him to endorse their shit. Yeah, I think you're right—he keeps winning, he's gonna be rich."

"So what do we do?"

Sol raised himself off the sofa and crossed the room to stare out of the window. A light from a streetlamp outside cast his dark skin in a yellow glow. He turned back around and faced Pinky. "I was out of the game—you know that, right? All the gang shit, it was all behind me. I'd done my bit. Fifteen years banging and I was done. Got respectable after that. We had the record label and the clothes and all that shit. Then, what happened to Bizness... I couldn't let that slide." He paused. "You know your Bible, younger?"

"Not really," he said.

"You should, blood. You don't have to be religious; still a lot of wisdom there. 'But if there is any further injury, then you shall appoint as a penalty life for life, eye for eye, tooth for tooth, hand for hand, foot for foot, burn for burn, wound for wound, bruise for bruise.' That's Exodus, man. Old school. That's the way I look at revenge, right there—you fuck me up, I'm going to fuck you up right back." Sol reached over and slapped Pinky on the back of the head. "You know I appreciate what you've done to help, younger. And you know I'm pleased you've brought this to me. This little pussy ran away, and he should've stayed hid. But he's back now, and he owes us."

"Course," Pinky replied, trying not to smirk at what he knew was coming.

Elijah had always been playing at the back of his mind. He had never liked the little pussy when they had hung out together on the estate, but JaJa had done something unforgivable that had never been paid back. There was that gym that the old man had set up, JaJa working out there like he was some big shot, and Pinky had called him out, told him that he was nothing, a pussy, that he couldn't fight, that Pinky could dook him out with one hand behind his back. It hadn't gone that way, though: Elijah had played with him, embarrassed him in front of the others, and, when he was done playing, he had banged him out. The moment was printed in Pinky's mind: he was on his hands and knees, saliva dripping out of his mouth, his mouth guard on the canvas, and the others all laughing at him. He had found JaJa in the week after Bizness had been killed and had threatened him. JaJa had told his mum, and his mum had called the police. Pinky had been arrested. The police had taken him out of the flat in cuffs. Pinky's mum had been there; she had had to watch it.

"When's he fighting next?" Sol asked, cutting through the toxic memories.

"Christmas Eve," Pinky said. "Someone called Connolly."

"Samuel Connolly?" he said. "From Tottenham?"

"You know him?"

Sol turned back to the darkened window. "A little. I knew his brother better. Tough kids."

"So what do we do?"

"Find out where Connolly trains, then come tell me. We need to have a little chat with him before the big night."

"And JaJa?"

"I got an idea for him, too," he said.

Pinky grinned. The day-to-day was interesting, but he'd been getting a little bored by how easy it all seemed. No one dared stand up to Sol, and they all knew that Pinky ran the operation around Blissett House. He wanted a challenge, and maybe this would be it. A chance to do something cool again.

And wipe that smile from the face of Little JaJa once and for all.

PART IV

THE NINTH DAY

6

Milton took his thick jacket down from the overhead bin and put it on. The weather had looked damp as they had circled to land, and now, as the passengers waited to descend the stairs to the tarmac, it felt as if the wind was running right through him. Gatwick was busy, with a constant stream of jets taking off and landing. It was just before midday, and the rain that greeted them was a gentle reminder of home.

Two days had passed since Milton had seen Elijah on the television. His next fight was scheduled for Christmas Eve, a week from now. Milton had dug up as much information on Elijah as he had been able to find. He had looked for an address, but had struck out. He would need to make enquiries in person if he was to pick up the scent.

Milton had just a single bag with him; it was all he had packed for his trip. He climbed into the transit bus and held onto the strap as the driver ferried them to the terminal. Once through arrivals—an easy thing to do despite the fact that the passport didn't bear his real name—Milton boarded the train that would take him into central London. He grabbed a free paper and skimmed it during the half-hour journey into Victoria. Christmas was soon, and the paper was full of seasonal advertisements. No one in the carriage with him looked particularly festive. It was cold and damp and the travellers were slumped into their seats, gazing out of the windows as they hurried through busy stations, watching the glum faces of the Londoners waiting for their own trains to arrive.

They arrived in the station. Milton disembarked and melted into the crowd that was queuing for the tube. Noise, smell and people all around: it was confirmation that he was back in the city. Milton had spent a month in much calmer surroundings, but now it was noise and people at every glance. A band from the Salvation Army had set up around a large Christmas tree, and, as Milton reached the downward escalator, they struck up with 'O Come, All Ye Faithful.'

The carol faded out as Milton descended. He took the Victoria Line to Oxford Circus, slowly negotiated the thronged station until he could change onto the Central Line, and then settled down as the train pulled out.

Bethnal Green had changed since the last time Milton had been here. It had always been a tough, hardscrabble sort of place, a hinterland on the fringes of the city in which hard men and tough women lived their lives in the shadow of the financial district. Its most famous sons were the Krays, the psychopathic gangsters who had ruled over its streets during the sixties. Then, it had been resolutely white and working class, full of straight-talking locals who had fought off both poverty and then the Luftwaffe, sticking two fingers up at the German bombers that had levelled whole streets.

Now, however, the fight against gentrification was evidently proving too much; Milton climbed out of the station to the street and saw the accoutrements of the money that had flowed in with the commuters who were increasingly making the borough their home: coffee shops selling artisanal beans, microbreweries, stationery shops selling leather-bound notebooks that cost fifty quid, warehouses that had been turned into comedy clubs and late-night bars.

Progress, Milton thought as he followed Cambridge Heath Road to the east. Not always to be celebrated.

Milton had reserved a room at the Town Hall Hotel. The building had once accommodated the authority for the borough of Bethnal Green and had been restored so that it was now a blend of historic architecture and contemporary verve. It was separated into two parts: the original town hall from the beginning of the twentieth century that faced Cambridge Heath Road, and the art deco extension from thirty years later that had housed the council chambers.

Milton made his way into the building, past the stained glass and wooden panelling from its recent past, and found the reception. It was a large, double-height room, and a tall Christmas tree had been set up in the space between the two flights of stairs, colourful presents laid out beneath its branches. A fire burned in the grate, and Christmas music was playing over the PA.

Milton went to check in.

"Mr. Smith," the woman behind the desk said after consulting her screen, "we've got you staying for a week."

"That's right," Milton said.

She encoded his key card, slipped it into a paper wallet,

and handed it to him. "Good news and bad news, I'm afraid. Bad news is that we've overbooked our standard rooms. The good news is that we've upgraded you to one of our suites. I hope that's all right?"

"Thank you very much," he said. "I'm sure that will be fine."

"You're on the ground floor," she said. "Room twelve. Enjoy your stay, Mr. Smith. And welcome to London."

7

Pinky had looked him up online. Connolly had had ten fights and had won all of them. Most of them looked like they were low-key—small crowds, no money—but the last two had been on the TV. He'd found them on YouTube, someone pirating the Sky Sports footage, and had decided that Connolly was all right. He was slow, didn't cover up well, but he had a big right hand that had knocked out half of the stiffs he'd been put up against. Ten fights, nine wins and a draw. Not bad.

He had put the word out on the street and had quickly tracked Connolly down to a gym in Tottenham. He had driven over there, nervous at being in the territory of another gang, and had sat in his car and waited for him to show up. He waited there until Connolly came outside again and then followed him, staying behind him and out of sight, a shadow that the man didn't know that he had. He followed him to a house and, from there, Pinky was able to fill out the details of his life: girlfriend, kid, where the girl worked, what they did with the kid in the day. Pinky got it all down, everything that Sol would need. He did a thorough job with his research and looked forward to delivering the information. Sol would be pleased with him. That wouldn't hurt at all.

There had been a lot of sitting around, and Pinky hadn't been able to resist digging into the background of Connolly's Christmas Eve opponent. He had taken out his phone and started to google.

Mustafa Muhammad.

Fucking JaJa.

He couldn't believe it was him. He'd watched all the videos that he could find. JaJa was bigger and stronger than he remembered, the skinny little runt filled out with muscle. He had fast hands and faster feet. Pinky could see that he had talent, and that made him grit his teeth in frustration. But he knew that JaJa would be the same little pussy underneath it all. He might have a bit of talent, but Pinky remembered how he had held him down in the playground and rubbed his head in dog shit. He remembered the look in JaJa's eyes, the fear that Pinky fed off, and he wanted to see it again.

PART V

THE EIGHTH DAY

8

Milton woke at five in the morning; the sky was still dark outside. He changed into a pair of black jeans, a black turtleneck shirt and his black Red Wing boots. He grabbed his jacket and left the hotel. It was cold outside—the forecasters were predicting an outside chance of snow for Christmas Day—and the residue from last night's grit was still scattered across the road. Milton took out his phone and opened his browser. There was a meeting of the Fellowship in a community centre that was just a short walk away from the hotel on Kedelstone Walk. He bought a coffee from a BP garage that he passed and followed his map to the centre, a single-storey building that had been built beneath the arches of the railway bridge that carried the trains into Liverpool Street.

There were a handful of people gathered outside the entrance to the community centre. Milton found himself thinking back to how he would have reacted to the prospect of going to a meeting the last time he was in East London. He knew that he would have waited at the periphery of the group and, more than likely, would have persuaded himself that it was a bad idea and left before the meeting had started. He would not have said that he was comfortable with the idea of attending the meeting, even now, but he knew that they were important to his recovery and that he always found peace in the sanctity of the rooms.

He nodded a greeting to the smokers who were finishing their cigarettes outside the building, and opened the door to go inside. The small meeting room had been prepared with four rows of chairs, and, as was his usual practice, Milton took a chair in the back row where he could keep a lower profile. There was a folding table at the front with two chairs behind it for the secretary and the speaker, and another table to the side held a collection of AA merchandise: new copies of the Big Book, associated texts and the plate that would be used to take the collection.

A banner had been unrolled and hung from the wall: it listed the Twelve Steps. Milton glanced at it, not really reading or taking it in, and found his thoughts drifting to Rutherford. He had met the old soldier at a meeting not all that far from here, and Rutherford had told him that he would get more out of the meetings if he participated. Milton had known then that Rutherford was right; he knew it now, too, and, although he occasionally spoke, especially when he found himself at his lowest ebb, most of the time he preferred to sit quietly and listen. He found the meetings to be the only place where he could clear his mind of the nagging voice that told him he was unworthy, that he had blood on his hands and that he would never be able to atone for the damage that he had done during his career. He listened to the speakers and focused on the similarities and not the differences. He would never find a story even remotely like his, but there were common threads that ran through each drunk's share: inadequacy, guilt, shame, regret, remorse.

The others filtered into the room and took their seats. There were fifteen of them, a decent turnout for an early morning meeting. The secretary took his seat and cleared his throat.

"My name is Andy," he said, "and I am an alcoholic."

Milton closed his eyes and listened.

9

The meeting finished at six. The others were going for breakfast at the greasy spoon nearby, but Milton politely declined the invitation to go along and made his way back to the hotel. He went back to his room and took a shower. He towelled himself down, dressed in the same clothes, and went for a breakfast of eggs and bacon and orange juice in the restaurant. There was a pile of newspapers on the side, and Milton took copies of the *Sun* and the *Times*. He turned to the back of the tabloid and thumbed through the sports section. Most of it was devoted to last night's football, but, just before the cartoons and crosswords, Milton found a short story on the upcoming fights. The focus was on the super-middleweights who were headlining the bill, but there was also a brief mention of the undercard, including a reference to Mustafa Muhammad. The young fighter was described as 'explosive' and an 'exciting talent.' Milton felt a fresh buzz of pride.

He finished a pot of coffee and went down the steps to the street outside. He flagged down a black cab and slid into the cabin.

"Where to?" the driver asked him through the open screen.

"Hackney," he said.

"Where in Hackney?"

"Do you know Blissett House?"

"I know it," he said. "Why'd you want to go there?"

"Nostalgia."

Milton sat back as they pulled out into the traffic. The cabbie tried to engage him in conversation, but, to his credit, he quickly realised from Milton's unenthusiastic responses that he would rather travel in silence. The man turned his attention back to the talk radio that he had been listening to.

They headed east, the new affluence of hipster Bethnal Green gradually replaced by crumbling high streets, shops and businesses struggling to make ends meet in the face of out-of-town malls and the internet. Charity shops had appeared where Milton remembered family businesses, and, as they continued farther east, even those became less and less frequent. Windows and doors were sealed with boards and metal grilles, the blandness alleviated only by the colourful gang tags that had been sprayed on the walls. The pedestrians that slouched along the pavements were a melting pot of ethnicities: Rastafarians with their dreads tied up and covered by knitted tams; Turks gathered outside their restaurants; Hasidic Jews, dressed all in black. The driver took them over a bridge that crossed the A12, traffic jammed up beneath it, then turned left into the estate that Milton remembered from before.

Not much had changed here; it might as well have been frozen in time. The convenience store still had metal bars across the windows, and, from the quick glimpse inside as they drove past, Milton could see that the cashier still sheltered behind a Plexiglas screen. He looked forward, out of the windscreen, and saw the three vast tower blocks that had seemingly sprouted from the grid of streets. He saw the names on the graffitied signs that announced them: Carson House, Howard House, Blissett House. They were still in poor condition; they had not been attended to in the interim. Milton found his thoughts running to Grenfell and the inferno that had fed on the cheap building materials within that building; thoughts of fire and death led him to the blaze in Sharon's flat, and the consequences that she now bore as a result of Milton's well-meaning but inept interference in her life.

The driver pulled up outside the tower block. Milton paid the fare, added a tip and got out. The cabbie didn't delay, turning around and disappearing in the direction from which they had just come.

Milton looked around. Memories came back to him: he remembered the house that he had lived in so that he could be close to Elijah and his mother; he remembered the hot and sultry summer, the pressure-cooker that had contributed to the violence that had swept out of Tottenham and across districts like this all across London.

It was colder now, and the sky was a leaden grey rather than the deep blue that he remembered, but the atmosphere felt the same. There was an oppressiveness as he looked up at the ugly block, with its chicken-coop flats, too many people living in close proximity to one another, pressed into a space that was too small for them, a building that had been neglected by the council, slowly rotting a little more every day.

He zipped up his leather jacket and started to walk.

10

It was ten in the morning and the courtyard at the foot of the block was quiet. Milton set off, walking by the red brick wall of a shed that housed the large industrial waste bins that served the building. The wall had become a canvas for gang tags. He saw the words FATSO and EMZEE and, over the top of them, black lettering that simply said LFB.

Milton remembered that, too.

LFB.

It stood for London Fields Boys.

He remembered Pops, the young man who had found himself unable to live with his conscience and who had been murdered for his honesty. He remembered the teenage boys, thirteen and fourteen and fifteen, who had caused such chaos in the estates. And he remembered Bizness, the charismatic rapper whom they all wanted to be, the Pied Piper who would have led the local boys away.

Milton took it all in, scanning his surroundings quickly and methodically as he always did. It was second nature to him now, a reflex that he didn't even notice. He looked for people who might be watching him, he looked for choke points and escape routes, all of it done in the blink of an eye. It had been three years, but it could have been three minutes. Nothing had changed, down to the same old detritus strewn outside. Burned-out cars, abandoned fridges and washing machines. Locals shuffled on the walkways overhead, and youngsters kept watch as they leaned against the railings.

Milton had thought about what he might do when he was putting the plan together in Tenerife. Blissett House had been the obvious place to start. He knew that Sharon and Elijah had moved on: Google said that Mustafa fought out of Sheffield. There had been nothing here for them before, and then Milton's meddling had made things worse. Sharon would have done anything to get Elijah somewhere safer.

Milton still wanted to go back.

He went into the piss-stinking lobby. The lift wasn't working, so he climbed the steps until he reached the sixth floor, where Elijah and his mum had once lived. Milton passed along the walkway. Some of the flats had Christmas decorations in the windows: tinsel drooping from one corner to the other, candleholders left on windowsills, fake snow sprayed across dusty panes. He walked on until he reached flat 609. He was depressed—but not particularly surprised—to find that the flat had not been repaired after the fire that had torn through it. A replacement front door was secured behind a heavy metal door that had been fitted to deter squatters. The windows were similarly protected, ugly orange metal boxes screwed into the frames. The brickwork, still blackened from the soot, bore the scars of the fire that had ripped through the flat. Milton thought, not for the first time, that it had been a miracle that the entire tower block hadn't gone up in flames.

He heard a noise from flat 607. He took a step back and set himself. The door opened a crack and then a face peered out. It was an elderly white woman; she looked him up and down, then made as if to shut the door again.

He recognised her: the Warriners' old next-door neighbour.

"Excuse me," Milton said, making his way towards the door. "I wonder if you can help me?"

"What do you want?" she demanded, speaking through the space between the door and the frame.

"I'm looking for someone who used to live here," Milton replied, keeping his tone jovial and straight. "Sharon Warriner?"

"Who are you? You the police?"

"No."

"Bailiff, then."

"Neither. Just an old friend. I've been away for a few years and wanted to get back in touch."

The door opened a little more, and the woman's full face came into view. She looked him up and down again, then shook her head. "Can't help you."

"Please," Milton said quickly, risking another step towards her. "I just want to see how they're doing now. I was around when the fire happened. I've just come back from working abroad, and I've misplaced the telephone number I had for Sharon."

The woman eyed him suspiciously. "They moved."

"To Sheffield?"

"Sorry," she said. Milton noticed her eyes flashing over his shoulder. "I don't know. Goodbye."

11

She shut the door; Milton heard her locking it and fastening the security chain. He turned to glance back in the direction that the woman had looked and saw four young men sauntering towards him along the walkway. They were nineteen or twenty, Milton guessed, older than most of the kids who had been hanging around in the open spaces at the foot of the block. They were all dressed in matching outfits—hoodies and jeans and white trainers—and had the same look of lazy, insouciant hostility.

Milton turned to face them. "What can I do for you?"

The tallest of the group was over six feet and heavily built. He stepped forward. "You lost?"

Milton checked them, one at a time, looking for any sign that they might have a knife. He could see the hands of the big man: they were empty. One of the others—just behind the first man and wearing a purple bandana—had his hand in his pocket. His face twitched, little tremors that might signal the anticipation of violence. Milton had seen that particular tell on many occasions before.

"I'm not lost," he said.

The man took him in, perhaps working out what he was going to do next.

"You're not the police?"

"I'm not."

"So what you doing outside JaJa's house? They ain't been there for years."

"I'm a family friend. I'm looking for him and his mother. Do you have a number for them?"

"I don't believe you," the man said. Milton tensed up as he reached into his pocket but, instead of the blade that Milton feared he might withdraw, he pulled out his phone. He held it up and took a picture of Milton.

"Don't do that," Milton said.

Milton heard the sound of the fake shutter as the man took his picture again.

"I asked nicely," Milton said.

"What?"

"I don't like having my picture taken."

He turned to his friends. "You hear that? He don't like having his picture taken."

He turned back to Milton and raised the phone as if to take another photo. Milton took a quick step forward, grabbed the man's arm with his right hand, and dug his fingertips into the soft, sensitive flesh on the underside of his wrist. The jolt of pain would have been sudden and severe, and Milton used it to force the man's arm down and then back, twisting it so that the man had no choice but to spin around. Milton pushed the man's hand up until it was right up between his shoulder blades. He took the phone from him.

"What you doing?" the man squealed. "That fucking hurts."

"I know," Milton said. He grasped the man's index and forefingers with his spare hand. "So does this."

Milton yanked down, bending the fingers just to the point before they would break.

The man yelled in pain. The other three were frozen, unsure whether they should move to help their friend or stay where they were. Milton had guessed right: the mouthy one was the leader, and the others were lost without him telling them what to do.

"What's the passcode?"

"Fuck you, lighty."

Milton yanked again.

"3926," he said.

Milton took the phone and, holding it one-handed, pressed the button to lock the screen, then tapped the screen to wake it. He entered the code with his thumb, and the phone unlocked. He put it into his pocket.

"Well done," Milton said. "Now—what's your name?"

"Little Mark."

"Your real name."

"Edwin."

"Thank you, Edwin. If your friends do anything silly, I'll snap your fingers. Understand?"

"Yes," he stammered.

"Tell them."

"Just... just stay where you are," he grunted as Milton gently increased the torque.

They did as they were told, all of them glaring at Milton with a mixture of hostility and surprise at what they were watching.

"Now, Edwin—do you know Elijah?"

"Yes. Used to. Back before."

"Before what?"

"The fire. His mum was burned."

"So where is he now?"

"He disappeared. They both did."

"Why did they do that?"

"There was a fight. Pinky threatened him and JaJa went to the police. Pinky got arrested. Police went to his flat and arrested him in front of his mum."

"And then?"

"Pinky got out and said he was gonna kill him."

Milton tweaked the fingers again; he could see that the other three were starting to wonder whether they ought to make a move on him, feeling a little strength in numbers, and he knew better than to outstay his welcome. He had them on the back foot, for now, but it wouldn't last.

"And?"

"And JaJa wasn't here no more. One day him and his mum were here; the next day they wasn't. No one knows where they went."

Milton pulled down on Edwin's index finger, almost to the breaking point. "What about now? Where are they now?"

"Sheffield," he grunted through the pain. "He's a boxer. He changed his name—Mustafa Muhammad. He's been up there. He's got a fight down here on Christmas Eve."

"Anything else?"

"That's it."

"Sure?"

"I swear it."

Milton quickly reached around with his spare hand and frisked the man. He felt the point of a blade in his pocket and pulled it out, glancing down to see a kitchen knife with a serrated edge.

"You should be careful," he said. "Carrying a knife around like that, you could easily get cut."

Milton held the edge of the blade against Edwin's throat and pulled him back to the railing, using him as a barrier as he negotiated the space between the edge of the walkway and the three young men, who were now clearly considering going for their own knives. Milton backed up all the way to the entrance to the stairwell.

"Who's Pinky?" Milton asked.

"He runs these ends."

"Where is he now?"

"I don't know," Edwin said. "Around."

"Tell him to stay away from Elijah. I've been nice to you. Friendly. I won't be friendly if I have to come around and tell him myself. Or if we have to speak again."

Milton took the knife away from Edwin's throat and slid it into his back pocket in the event that he might need it on the way out of the block. He held onto the man's wrist and grabbed the back of his jacket with his left hand, pulling him back half a step, and then drove him forward so that his head crashed into the concrete door frame. Edwin grunted and Milton felt his knees loosen; he pivoted, shoving him into the other boys, who were still watching, their mouths agape.

Milton turned into the stairwell and started down, moving quickly but not too quickly. There was no sound of pursuit; Milton took the knife, wiped his prints from the handle, and tossed it into the open bin as he made his way past it and back out into the courtyard. He looked back up to the sixth floor and saw four faces looking down at him: three were confused, and the fourth was twisted in pain.

Milton headed back to the main road. He reached into

his pocket, leaving Edwin's phone and taking out his own. He opened his texts and sent a message. He was going to need a little help.

12

Pinky waited in the car for the signal. He had parked outside the gym and was scowling at it through the film of rainwater that sluiced down the windshield. It was a foul evening, and Pinky would have much rather stayed in his flat than drive all the way across town to Tottenham. Apart from the inconvenience, it was *dangerous*. If the Tottenham Mandem or the Northumberland Park Killers knew he was here, in their postcode, there was a good chance they would come after him.

The last thing he needed was beef. It made him anxious, and it irritated him that Sol had insisted that he drive him. Pops had used to be the same, talking down to him, telling him what to do, and look what had happened there. Pinky looked in the mirror and watched Sol in the back seat of the Range Rover. Pinky closed his focus and looked at his own reflection. *That's right*, he thought. *Didn't go well for Pops at all.*

"Boy's still inside," Sol said.

Pinky looked across the pavement to the gym. Sol had two youngers standing near the entrance. Good boys who did as they were told. Little Mark was in a BMW parked around the corner, waiting to move. Seeing Little Mark reminded him of what he had told him earlier: that an older white man had caused trouble at Blissett House. Mark hadn't told him anything other than that, and now Pinky was worried about the police or the Albanian gangs who were starting to look at pushing their gear into territories that had previously been off limits to them. He would have to tell Sol, but he wanted to find out more before he did that.

Pinky tapped a hand on the steering wheel in time with the beat of the new Stormzy track and kept the beat as it switched to Skepta. The bass throbbed. The cabin smelled of weed; Sol had been smoking all the while as they had headed northwest.

"There," Sol said. "There he is."

The door opened and a young guy with a sports holdall slung over one shoulder emerged onto the street. The two youngers fell into step behind him. Pinky saw the door to Little Mark's BMW open.

"What are you waiting for?" Sol said.

"What?"

"Go get him!"

"That wasn't what we said—"

"Just go get him, a'ight?"

Pinky got out of the car, the rain slamming into his face. Sol didn't want to treat him like this, like he was some sort of nobody, like one of the police who dribbled down their chins after one too many idiot pills. He knew he wasn't an equal, not yet, but he was different to the youngers, different to Little Mark, and being treated like this wasn't what he had in mind. He bit down his frustration, wiped the rain from his eyes, and started towards the gym. Little Mark was closing in. The youngers—seventeen years old, big for their age and with bad attitudes—shouted something, causing Connolly to look over his shoulder. He stopped and turned around to face them as they closed in.

Pinky watched and waited.

Connolly dropped the holdall and moved quickly, knowing what was coming before any words were exchanged. He closed the space to the taller of the two youngers quickly and grabbed his left arm, smashing his forearm into the side of the kid's head. The younger dropped like a stone, leaving the other kid backing away.

Fucking amateurs.

Pinky shouted Little Mark's name.

Connolly moved towards the second younger, his fist cocked, shouting something that was lost in the rush of the rain. Little Mark moved quickly. He was onto Connolly before he had even realised that he was there. Mark was a good six inches taller and fifty pounds heavier; he hooked one burly arm under Connolly's armpit and the other across his throat.

Pinky reached into his pocket and took out his butterfly knife. He reached Connolly, still wrestling with Little Mark, and flicked his wrist so that the blade snicked out. He grabbed Connolly by the scruff of the neck and held out the blade so that he could see it.

"Get in the car," he said, nodding to the Range Rover.

Pinky held the knife inches from Connolly's nose. The boxer eyed it. "Who the fuck are you?" he grunted.

"We just want to talk, that's all. Get in."

Pinky led the way back to the Range Rover and opened the rear door. Connolly must have realised that he was outnumbered, and he calmed down enough for Little Mark to shepherd him to the back of the car. Mark put his hand on Connolly's head and pushed him down, then shoved him into the cabin. Pinky got in next to him, pressing Connolly up against Sol. Mark shut the door.

"Hello, Samuel," Sol said.

Pinky turned his head and looked at Connolly. He was smaller than he'd expected, about the same height as him; he might not have been all that tall, but his chest and arms were thick with muscle. His nose was squashed and bent to one side and his tight black braids were wet from the rain.

"Who the fuck are you?" said Connolly.

"Solomon Brown. You can call me Sol."

Connolly's face flickered with recognition. He had run with the Tottenham Mandem as a younger, although he had made a big song and dance about how he was "out of all that" and "saved by his boxing," chatting the shit that the white guys in suits probably told him he had to say if he was going to have a chance to make it out in the mainstream. He knew enough about the life that Solomon Brown's name would have meant something to him.

"What do you want?" he asked.

"You got a fight coming up," he said. "Christmas Eve, right?"

"Yeah—so?"

"I need you to do me a favour, Samuel."

Connolly shook his head. "No," he said. "*No fucking way.*"

"You don't know what I'm going to ask you yet."

"You're gonna ask me to throw the fight. No way, man. I ain't doing that. You don't know what I had to do to get to where I am."

Sol shuffled around in the seat so that he could put his hand on Connolly's shoulder. "Samuel—"

"I'm not throwing no fight, man," Connolly said quickly, his voice thick with anger. "I beat Muhammad, I get a shot at a belt. You know how much that's worth? You couldn't pay me enough to give that up."

"Everything has its price."

"Not this. It's not money. It's status."

"Who said I was talking about money?" Sol glanced over at Pinky. "Show him."

Pinky kept his knife in his left hand, making sure that Connolly could see it, and took out his phone. He used his thumb to open his photos and videos, selected one that he had shot earlier, and hit play. Pinky had shot the footage through the window of his car. He had parked on Bounds Green Road, riding the car up the kerb so that the wheels were half on the pavement and half in the road. The Co-Operative Childcare Nursery was on the corner of the road, and Pinky had filmed the little kids in their fluorescent tabards as they were led back inside from a trip to the park. He didn't know which kid was Connolly's, but he could tell from the boxer's reaction when the girl or the boy was in shot.

"Come on," Connolly said. His voice was tight, a little hoarse, and his fists were clenched in his lap.

"Like I said, it don't have to be about money, but there's no need for it to be unpleasant, neither." Sol patted Connolly on the knee. "This is how it's gonna be. You're gonna let yourself get hit in the third round, and you're gonna go down, and you're not gonna get up until they count ten. You get me? The third round. Down you go."

Connolly didn't answer.

"I'm going to put some money on you, Samuel, *mad* money, and if I lose that money because you don't do what you've been told to do, I'm gonna send my friend here to the nursery, or maybe to your house. We know where you live, Samuel. We know about Ayana, too—where she works, where she gets her nails done. And your folks. We know it all."

Connolly stiffened but didn't say anything; Pinky could see that Sol had scared him. There was something about the way he spoke—the contradiction of his calm, measured tone and the threats he was making—that gave him that edge that was so frightening.

"Like I said," Sol went on, "it don't need to be unpleasant between us. You go down in the third round and I'm gonna get paid. When I do, I'm going to make sure you get a little taste of that, too. My friend here, he's gonna bring you ten grand for your troubles."

"*Ten?*" Connolly said before laughing bitterly. "When I beat Muhammad, I'll make a *million*."

"But that's not going to happen, Samuel. You don't have to take it. That's up to you. But I need to make something really clear—you're not going to beat him. You go down when I tell you to go down. I need you to tell me you understand."

Connolly's fists clenched and unclenched, but he didn't speak. Pinky flicked his wrist again and the blade sprang out of the knife. He rested the point of the blade against Connolly's leg, at the side of the knee. He kept the blade sharp and he knew from experience that it wouldn't take much to slide it through the thin fabric and into the skin, and not much more than that to slice into the fat and the muscle beneath. He swallowed in anticipation, knowing that they couldn't mark Connolly now, not before the fight: everything would go to shit if they hurt him so badly that it was all called off. He slowly withdrew the blade and flicked it shut again, hoping that Sol would give him licence to come back and see Connolly again.

Sol spoke slowly and clearly. "Samuel—tell me. You *do* understand, don't you?"

He nodded.

"Good. Now fuck off."

He nodded and Pinky opened the car and stepped outside into the rain again. He motioned for Connolly to get out, and the man slid across the seat and stepped onto the pavement, his face a mask of hatred. Little Mark was standing with his back to the wall of a nearby building, rain dripping off the brim of his Raiders cap, his hoodie pulled up over his head. Pinky nodded to him, sending him on his way, and got back into the driver's seat of the Range Rover.

He pulled out, leaving Connolly to stare at them from the side of the road.

"Boy knows who we are and what we do," Sol said. "He's gonna do what he needs to do. Our boy gets the win he needs and we make some cash. Just a little taste of what we *will* make, though. JaJa's gonna make sure of that."

PART VI

THE SEVENTH DAY

13

Milton sat down at the bench table in the window of the Starbucks outside Liverpool Street station. He had two cappuccinos and a croissant laid out in front of him. He sipped his coffee, removed the plastic lid, and then dunked the pastry into it. He had been for a run around Victoria Park that morning and hadn't had time for breakfast after his shower. He had an appointment to keep, and the value of the information that he was expecting to receive meant that he didn't want to be late.

He had finished the croissant by the time he saw the man making his way across the concourse towards the coffee shop. He was short, with a nest of untidy ginger hair that spilled out from beneath a faded denim cap. His eyes were a little bulbous, bulging out above sallow cheeks that rarely saw the sun. His complexion was pale. He was wearing a surplus military coat, drab olive with a dirty fur collar, a pair of ripped jeans with a keychain that dangled all the way down to his knee, and a pair of scuffed Dr Martens boots. He had a rucksack slung over his shoulder.

His name was Ziggy Penn, and Milton hadn't seen him since he had helped him rectify the unpleasantness that Milton had found in Manila. Ziggy had once been employed by the Firm, just as Milton had, and had been seconded to Group Fifteen to act as an analyst and to provide technical backup on operations. He had worked with Milton on several occasions: a job against terrorist fundraisers in New Orleans, the situation with the Russian sleepers in Winchester and, after Milton had left the Group, the freelance jobs in Manila and Tel Aviv.

Ziggy came inside and walked over to the window.

"Milton," he said.

Milton gave Ziggy the spare cappuccino and indicated that he should sit down. He had left a message for Ziggy on a forum that was dedicated to the music of Morrissey and the Smiths. Ziggy was paranoid about security and had never given Milton any other way to contact him. He monitored the board, or had some algorithm that monitored it for him, and whenever he saw the trigger message, he would initiate proper contact.

"Thanks for coming," Milton said.

"Yes, well, you owe me. Things have been a little—" he paused "—hairy lately. I haven't been outside the hotel for a week. Keeping a low profile."

"What have you been doing?"

He winked. "Never you mind. I think the moment has passed, though. And I haven't seen you for ages. Much better to catch up in person."

Ziggy never really explained what he spent his time doing, although Milton's experience of him suggested that his near-constant paranoia might be justified. Ziggy was a skilled hacker, operating in the margins of the legitimate internet and the dark web, and Milton had no doubt that his ethical flexibility when it came to his work would have left victims all around the world. There had been several times when Ziggy had found himself in hot water and in need of Milton's assistance: the time, for example, when Milton had been required to extricate him from the clutches of a Japanese Yakuza after he had been persuaded to help him find and steal quarter-million-dollar supercars in Tokyo. Ziggy had a lot of expensive kit and no obvious means of paying for any of it; Milton didn't have to be a genius to conclude that he funded his lifestyle by illicit means.

"What do you have for me?" Milton said.

Ziggy sipped the coffee and then looked down at the pastry crumbs on the table. "You didn't get me one?"

"I'll get you a croissant when you tell me what you've got."

"No gratitude," he grumbled, opening his rucksack and taking out a MacBook. The lid was embossed with colourful decals: WikiLeaks, FSociety, the Guy Fawkes logo of Anonymous, an ersatz Intel logo that said, instead, 'Hacker Inside.' He opened the lid and tapped a key to wake up the computer.

"All right," he said. "You want to tell me why you're suddenly so interested in a boxer?"

"I knew him once," Milton said. "He's done well for himself—I'd like to see him and shake his hand."

"And?"

"And I want to make sure he's all right. I tried to help him out. He was in a difficult situation—him and his mother. I went to their old flat and they're not there. Apparently, they just disappeared."

"Yes," Ziggy said. "It looks like they did. Three years ago. I found all his old social media accounts—Snapchat, Facebook, even his YouTube credentials—he killed them all the same evening. His mother, too. Looks like they tried to wipe their history."

"But not so that you couldn't find it?"

"That would be impossible," Ziggy said, snorting at the preposterousness of Milton's suggestion. "There are always traces. Little threads that you can find—pull on them until you find another, pull on that until you track them down. They moved to a hostel in south London first of all. The place has its records online, and I found details for both Elijah and Sharon Warriner. They stayed there for a week; then they went to Margate. Stayed there for two years. They changed their names: Sharon and Elijah became Adara and Mustafa Muhammad. It would appear that they converted to Islam—I found evidence that they both attended the Al-Birr mosque. And Elijah—*Mustafa*—started working out at the Isle of Thanet Amateur Boxing Club."

That chimed with what Milton had been able to find out. The reports that he had read from the start of Elijah's amateur career said that he fought out of that club. He had risen through the amateur rankings quickly, fighting regularly in the years since he'd left London.

"And then they went to Sheffield," Milton said.

"A year ago. Turns out he won a place at the national performance centre. I don't know a lot about boxing, but this place is for the best, when they think someone's going to be good enough to fight at the Olympics, that sort of level. Anthony Joshua trained there."

Milton nodded. He knew: you didn't get an invitation to train there unless you had the potential to be seriously good. The thought of the progress Elijah had made filled Milton with pride, even if his involvement had been limited to introducing Elijah to the sport.

"The centre took his profile down after he went pro, but it was easy to find. Here."

He turned the laptop around so that Milton could read it:

Mustafa first became interested in boxing after a friend suggested he had potential. He quickly showed a natural ability for boxing and at age seventeen he won the England Boxing National Junior title, which he followed up a year later by winning the England Boxing Junior and Youth National Championships. His success in the junior and youth ranks translated to the seniors, and he won the first of his two England Boxing Elite National Championship titles a year later.

"The friend who thought he had potential?" Ziggy said. "Is that you?"

Milton thought of Rutherford. "Probably someone else."

Milton read on. Elijah had turned professional soon after his eighteenth birthday and was now nineteen years old and about to have the biggest fight of his career.

"Anything else?"

"I found their financial details," he said. "Useful?"

"*Shit*, Ziggy," Milton said, momentarily annoyed at Ziggy's intrusiveness, and then, deciding that it was relevant, he changed his mind. "Go on, then."

"Sharon has been working three jobs, from the looks of things. She's been receiving wages from Sheffield High School for Girls and Blades Domestic Cleaning Agency. She also works in a call centre in the evenings. She has £653 in a Halifax current account, but she does have another £14,832 in an ISA with Lloyds. Her credit rating is poor, and she's been turned down for loans on three separate occasions." He tapped the mouse and brought up another screen. "Elijah has made around £25,000 as a boxer. I've been able to trace payments into his account a day or two after each fight that he's had. But he doesn't have much to show for it."

"Not many get rich with boxing," Milton said. "The money's poor unless you're really good, and it's expensive. He'll need to pay his trainer, gym time, sparring partners, travel."

"Lots of outgoings. Looks like he's been helping his mum with the rent and food, too, and that fourteen thousand she's saved has been topped up every time he fights. He's giving what little he has left to her."

"You got their address?" he asked.

"Of course. They're renting a two-bedroom flat on White Thorns Close in Batemoor."

"Well done," Milton said.

"Anything else?"

Milton took out the phone that he had taken from the young man in Blissett House. "Could you analyse this for me?"

"Sure. Passcode?"

"3926," Milton said.

"How'd you get that? Ask nicely?"

"Something like that," he said.

"I don't want to know. What am I looking for?"

"I was jumped by four young men in Hackney. I took this from one of them. They belong to a gang—the London Fields Boys. Get me whatever you can. Phone numbers for the rest of the gang. Photos. Where they hang out. Anything that might be helpful."

"Leave it with me," Ziggy said, putting the phone into his bag. "What's next?"

Milton got up. "Sheffield," he said. "Can you look up the station I need for the train?"

"What am I? Your travel agent?"

Milton gestured down at the open laptop. "I'm sorry. It was just—"

"You'd be wasting your time," he said.

"But you said—"

"I know what I said. They *live* there, but they're not there *now*."

"So?"

"They're on the A1(M), just north of Luton."

"How do you..." He let the sentence drift. "Right. You got into their phones."

"First thing I did. But that's not how I found out. You know your friend has a website?"

"Of course," Milton said. "I looked at it yesterday."

"You don't know he updated it late last night?"

Ziggy pointed to the screen, which showed Mustafa Muhammad's website. There was an image on the front page that hadn't been there when Milton had checked before: Elijah and his opponent were in profile, glaring at each other. A line of logos below identified some of the companies who were involved in the fight: StubHub, William Hill, Sky Sports, Showtime, Matchroom Boxing. In the middle of the screen, between the two expressionless faces, was a banner that announced a public workout in three days at 6 p.m. at York Hall in Bethnal Green.

Ziggy tapped a finger against the screen. "You can go and say hello yourself."

14

York Hall was empty. Elijah had fought here four times before and he loved it. It was a medium-sized space with a vaulted barrel roof that had a series of skylights right down the middle. The ring had been set up in the middle of the floor, with temporary plastic seating installed around it. There were eight rows of seating in the circle above, and a large overhead light was suspended from the ceiling.

This was the last spar before the public workout, but it was no less difficult than the first. There had been long weeks of training in the lead-up to the fight, but, in reality, Elijah had never stopped working since the first moment he'd put on gloves in the Margate gym.

Elijah waited as his trainer, McCauley, adjusted his headgear and then slapped him on the shoulder. The sparring partner in the opposite corner was waiting. His name was Miroslav and he had been picked to mimic Samuel Connolly's style. Miroslav was shorter and stockier than Elijah, an inside fighter who would target his body, softening him up for hooks to the head in later rounds. That was what McCauley was expecting Connolly to do. The only difference was that it would be in front of eight thousand people rather than in a cold gym with just a handful of onlookers.

Elijah knew. *This* would be his moment.

York Hall was a long way from the spit and sawdust of the East London gym where he had started out. McCauley was more modern in his methods than Rutherford, the man who had taken him in under his wing first of all. He had been a scared fifteen-year-old then, with no idea that he would be able to box. The prospect of hurting people had made him uncomfortable, just as that hot summer as an awkward member of the LFB had made him uncomfortable, too. He didn't have to think too long to take himself back there again: Pops, shot in the park; Milton, the man who had saved him and his mother and then abandoned him; Rutherford, the first person to really invest in him. His memories always followed the same course, like a river running to its inevitable conclusion: he always ended up in the gym, going back because Rutherford had never turned up with the takeaway curry that he'd said he was going to bring for them to eat. He remembered seeing Rutherford on the floor, his arms and legs spread wide, a gunshot wound to the head, and Milton nowhere to be found.

The buzzer sounded and Elijah went to work.

Miroslav was from Eastern Europe, didn't speak a word of English, but knew what he was being paid to do and did it well. They met in the centre of the ring, Elijah throwing out a jab, landing on the cheek piece of the older man's head-gear. He threw another jab, then slipped to the side, using his footwork to create distance between them. He fired out another straight jab that was caught on Miroslav's glove, and then fired a hook into his other arm.

"Double up on the jab," McCauley shouted from the corner. "Keep working."

Elijah heard his voice, registered it, but kept his concentration on the bigger man in front of him. He watched the way he was moving and began to see someone other than the pale Hungarian or Pole or whatever he was; instead, he saw a black man, black braids, a squashed nose. He saw someone who had grown up in similar streets to him, someone who had known the life that Elijah had known as a younger, someone who had lived through the same shit day after day, someone who was good with his fists and was going to use them to get out, to make something of his life, just like him.

He saw someone who wanted to escape the past as much as Elijah did.

There was no let-up. Elijah continued to work, using his longer arms to try to keep Miroslav from getting too close to him, picking him off at range the way a matador taunts a bull, ducking out of the way when he came in swinging. He pivoted left and right, ducked, arched backwards so the crosses and hooks missed by inches, making Miroslav miss and miss and miss.

The buzzer sounded.

Elijah went back to his corner. McCauley sat him down on the stool and splashed water in his face.

"Let him in now. One round—let him get inside. Cover up and look for counters. Let him work for a little, then use your footwork to move off the ropes. Don't look for bombs. That comes later, when he's tired himself out."

Elijah nodded, opening his mouth so that McCauley could spray a jet inside, then spitting it out over the ropes.

The buzzer sounded again and he beckoned Miroslav towards him once more.

He tucked his elbows into his sides, put his chin down against his sternum, and took the shots that Miroslav was trying to land on his arms. He didn't feel the pain; the adrenaline was buzzing through him now. He knew that Connolly's punches would be harder, more brutal, the gloves smaller and more impactful.

He saw an opening and took it. There was a moment's pause, and Miroslav's left hand dropped down from covering his chin for a split second. It was as if time slowed down: Elijah saw the move and made the decision without even thinking about it. Elijah knew that Miroslav was hard as nails. He weighed a stone more than Elijah, and now he felt the weight of him leaning against his body. Tough to shift, tough to slip away from when they were that close, wearing him down with his weight.

None of that mattered: Elijah landed an uppercut to his chin and the world stopped. He felt the impact through his arm. Even wearing sixteen-ounce gloves, the force Elijah had been able to generate was enough to make Miroslav wilt.

Elijah moved away as Miroslav went down on one knee. He could hear McCauley saying something from the corner, but he paid no attention to it. It was drowned out by the noise in his head, the thousands of people chanting his name. He looked down, and the stocky white man at his feet was young and black. He looked out and saw the flashes from cameras, the MC stepping through the ropes, a microphone in his hand.

Elijah knew it. He was certain of it.

He was going to win.

15

McCauley unlaced Elijah's gloves and took them off, then checked his hands for injuries. Elijah wiped sweat from his brow and waited. McCauley had been his trainer since he'd been an amateur, following him when he turned pro, and he knew him better than anyone else. His face was unreadable. McCauley was twenty-five years older than Elijah, but he seemed even older.

"See that uppercut?" Elijah said, grinning as he remembered the impact. "That's gonna get Connolly out of there."

McCauley nodded but didn't reply, concentrating on checking Elijah's face for marks or cuts. A nick would have ended it all for now, but McCauley didn't say anything, so Elijah concluded that he must be fine.

"I brought him in, like you said, let him wear himself out, then I let go with it. Right? Tagged him on the chin. I hit him with that when I'm wearing the eight-ounce gloves and he'll be out cold before he hits the floor."

McCauley started to unwrap the tape from around Elijah's hands. There would be more work later, but, for that moment, Elijah could only think of that impact. Of the power he could generate and of the knockout that was going to follow. The statement he would make.

"What you think?" Elijah said. "You ain't said nothing."

"I think you're getting too cocky," McCauley said, his voice low and flat. "We can't have that for this one. He's no chump."

"I just know what I can do," Elijah replied, standing up and flicking his arms out, lightly shadow-boxing. "Ain't nothing but confidence. You told me that was important."

"Confidence is good, Mustafa. Arrogance gets you knocked out."

"It ain't arrogant when you can back it up."

"You've had nine fights. Connolly's a boxer you should be facing in ten fights' time, not now. You can beat him, but you've got to remember to be humble. Win this and win it well, and we don't look back. Lose it and all our hard work is wasted. Understand?"

McCauley was serious; Elijah knew not to mess with him when he was in this kind of mood. "I understand."

McCauley grabbed his face with both hands and stared into his eyes. "You're not going to lose as long as you stay focused. Right?"

"Right," Elijah said.

McCauley patted him on the cheek. "Good boy. Now—what about tonight?"

"What about it?"

"You forgot?"

Elijah remembered. "The press conference. Shit."

The night's action was going to be broadcast on Sky, and they wanted their pound of flesh; that meant that all the fighters on the bill were contractually obliged to appear at a televised conference at the Courthouse Hotel in Soho.

Elijah would have preferred to spend the night in his room, but McCauley had made it plain that there was no avoiding it.

"I know it's a pain," he said now, "but it's part of the business. Get used to it. Just for an hour, that's it. Answer the questions, be respectful; then we can go and get something to eat. All right?"

Elijah said that he would be there. McCauley started to clean up and left Elijah to work out for another hour, shadow-boxing around the ring until the overhead lights were switched off. He went through to the back and showered. He wrapped a towel around his waist and looked in the mirror of the ancient changing room. He looked good: one hundred and thirty pounds of muscle, lithe and toned, with lightning-fast reflexes and power. He flashed out a combination, right-left-right-left, ending with a right hook that would lift Connolly out of his boots when he landed it at the fight.

16

Milton went to the Rio cinema in Dalston that afternoon. They were showing *It's A Wonderful Life*, and he took his place in an audience of pensioners and students and allowed himself to be drawn away. But afterward, he left the auditorium with a wistfulness that he would, as usual, be spending Christmas on his own. That had been the way of it for most of his adult life. He remembered his time in the army fondly and remembered one particular Christmas more clearly than the others. He had been in the SAS, sent out to Belize for jungle-warfare training. They had come out of the jungle to visit the nearest town, and had watched the local Garifuna community take to the street to enjoy the Jankunu dancers. He remembered the masked and costumed dancers parading the main street, roaming from house to house and accompanied by the rhythmic beat of traditional drummers.

His time in the Group had not afforded him similar experiences, and, especially towards the end of his career, he had been drinking so much as to have obliterated the memories. Since he had withdrawn from government service, he had always spent the holidays alone. His long sojourn had included festive stops in the Americas and Eastern Europe, and several in London. Alex Hicks had invited him last year; Milton had declined and had, instead, worked at the taximen's shelter where he had been employed on and off whenever he found himself in the city. He had decided to stay in Tenerife this year, and had a return flight booked immediately after the conclusion of the fights on Christmas Eve.

He didn't mind. He had long since decided that he was best alone, that the occasional stab of loneliness was a useful reminder of what he had done, the reason why he didn't deserve anything else.

This year would be no different.

MILTON RETURNED to the hotel and settled down in his room. He checked his watch: it was just before eight. The press conference was being broadcast via the promoter's account on YouTube. Milton took out his phone and stood it against the vase on the table. He poured boiling water into a Pot Noodle that he had bought at the convenience store on his way back from the cinema and then sat down to watch. The conference was being held at a hotel in central London. A large canvas backdrop had been erected with pictures of all of the fighters set out across it. The headline bout was between James Cullum and Vasily Yankovich, and those fighters were arranged on either side of the young promoter. There were eight other fighters, arranged across two desks, one raised up higher than the other one. A small crowd of onlookers were visible at the bottom of the shot, some of them holding their phones aloft so that they could record the proceedings.

Milton saw Elijah straight away. He was sitting on the left-hand side of the lower desk, wearing a grey hoodie and a black cap with a logo that Milton was unable to read. His name—Mustafa Muhammad—was displayed on a nameplate that had been positioned on the desk in front of his microphone. His opponent was sitting on the other side of the desk, separated by two middleweights and a bantamweight. The nameplate said Samuel Connolly; the young boxer was wearing a bright yellow hoodie, his skin a little lighter than Elijah's, his hair cropped tight against his scalp.

Milton put the fork into the pot, loaded it with noodles, and slotted it into his mouth. He had eaten earlier, and this snack was just to take the edge off his hunger before he went out for his second run of the day.

The promoter, noted on screen as Tommy Porter, tapped the microphone and brought the proceedings to order.

"Good evening, everyone," he said. "Thanks for coming down to Shoreditch in London today. So—this card, announced last month, is going to be a Christmas cracker. It's almost sold out, but the good news is that it'll be live and exclusive on Sky Sports. Five great fights, all complete fifty-fifties, televised from eight o'clock and then going on through the night. We'll get to the mouth-watering super-middleweight contest at the top of the bill last of all, but, before then, we're going to hear from these young men around me, all of them electrifying prospects, from featherweights to heavyweights. We're going to start with Dwayne Craig, who, for my money, is the best cruiserweight prospect I've seen in this country for ten years. Dwayne—you're licking your lips after seeing a brilliant cruiserweight fight last week between Bruce and Hadley."

The cruiserweight to Elijah's left started to talk about how he was looking forward to getting in the ring, how his rivals had been hiding from him for too long, and how he was going to knock out his opponent within three rounds, the usual flannel that was a stock-in-trade of these kinds of events.

Milton tuned it out, watching Elijah instead.

17

Pinky was in one of the LFB flats in Blissett House. The usual crew was there, smoking and drinking and jawing about the old guy who had robbed Little Mark of his phone outside JaJa's burned-out old flat the day before. Pinky had sat down with Little Mark and the other boys and had got him to describe exactly what had happened. Mark was embarrassed; he was big, and his whole rep was built on how hard he was. From what Pinky had been told, he had been manhandled by the older guy, had his phone nicked, and then been forced to give up the passcode. All four of them had gotten a good look at the old guy: he was average looking, around six feet tall, wiry. His hair was messy, needing a cut, a frond curling across his forehead. There was a scar across his face, so faint as to be almost impossible to see. They had all commented on his eyes: icy blue, cold, and frightening.

Pinky had paused at that, remembering the man with freaky blue eyes who had taken out Bizness on the night of the riots. He remembered him, and he wondered: JaJa was coming back, and maybe that man was back, too. He thought about it, thought about telling Sol, but he decided against it. It couldn't be him.

"Hey!" Kidz called out. "Look at this!"

The flat-screen TV that they had fixed to the wall was showing a YouTube stream of a live event. Pinky looked: ten young men, mostly black, and a well-dressed white guy, all sitting before a big canvas with their pictures on it. The caption at the bottom of the screen said that it was a press conference, and that it was broadcasting from London.

"Is this on now?" Pinky asked.

"It's live," Kidz said. "It's him, isn't it? It's JaJa."

There was no question about it. The nameplate before him read Mustafa Muhammad, but it was Elijah. Pinky would have recognised him anywhere.

"Why'd he change his name?" Little Mark said.

"Religion. He's a Muslim now."

"*Bullshit*," Pinky sneered. "He changed his name because he didn't want to be found; same reason he disappeared."

The younger in the corner turned up the Bluetooth speaker so that the new 1011 tune boomed through the flat.

"Turn that shit down," Pinky yelled.

The younger did as he was told, and Kidz found the remote and increased the volume on the TV. The white man in the expensive suit and the open-necked shirt was speaking.

"Before we get to the championship fight, we've got a ten-round match featuring one of the hottest prospects in the sport of boxing. It might be the fight I'm looking forward to most of all. Mustafa Muhammad is British boxing's best-kept secret. He's nineteen years old, and he's already fought nine times since he turned pro. The reason he's managed to fit that many fights into his young career is because no one's got past the third round with him, and practically no one has landed a glove on him. He's got

his biggest test on Christmas Eve, putting his record on the line against Tottenham's Samuel Connolly. We'll hear from Samuel in a moment, but, Mustafa, first of all, tell us how you see the fight going for you. What's the difference between the two of you?"

"There's one big difference," Elijah said. *"When he hits someone, they get up. When I hit someone, they're unconscious. There's a big difference between my punching power and his."* He closed his fist. *"He's got rockets. I got nuclear bombs."*

One of the youngers whooped as Elijah looked into the camera and kissed his closed fist.

"Look at that little pussy," Pinky said. "Thinks he's better than all the rest of them."

"That's because he is," Kidz said. "You watched any of his fights?"

"Some," Pinky said. "There's highlights on YouTube."

"They're all there," he said. "The full fights. Check them out. I know you don't like him, Pinky, but, seriously, he's got mad skills."

The younger came up closer to the TV, edging next to Pinky. "I watched them," he said. "There's this one fight, this dude from Brixton, Mustafa just nailed him with—"

"His name's *JaJa*," Pinky spat, cuffing the boy around the head with the back of his hand. "And, anyway, shut the fuck up. You speak when you're spoken to, a'ight?"

The younger frowned, biting down on his lip, and Pinky wondered if he was going to cry. He ignored him. He stared at JaJa and felt the familiar flickering of his temper. There was no forgetting and no forgiving what he had done. Seeing Elijah there—on the TV, doing well for himself, people fawning over him—just brought it all back again. Pinky would see that Elijah paid for what he had done. He hadn't had the chance before, but now *he* was someone, too.

This time it would be different.

18

Elijah was told by someone from Tommy Porter's team that he would have to stick around after the conference to have his photo taken. He waited in line as the other fighters were arranged on a platform, standing face-to-face as the assembled press photographers did their work. Most of the fighters were respectful of each other, shaking hands or pumping fists as they went about their business. Elijah thought about what McCauley had told him and made an effort to rein back the braggadocio that he had allowed to get the better of him during the conference. He thought of what his mother would say, and how she would have told him to treat his opponent with the respect that he would want to be treated with himself.

Connolly hopped up onto the platform and waited for Elijah to join him. Porter came forward, offering Elijah his hand.

"That was great," he said. "You've got a lot of charisma. They'll love that."

Elijah nodded and climbed up onto the platform. Connolly looked at him, but, as Elijah held his gaze, the older man looked away. Elijah frowned; that wasn't what he had expected. Connolly was well known as a hard man, and McCauley had warned him that he would try to make him feel small. That hadn't happened at all.

"Let's have some attitude," Porter urged.

Elijah felt uncomfortable, but he knew that boxing was show business, and he was in the business of putting on a show. He raised both fists and stared at Connolly and frowned again at his reluctance to reciprocate.

"Come on, Sam," Porter said. "Give it some."

Connolly looked up, closed his own fists and held them in a loose guard. Elijah stared at him, but Connolly still would not hold his eye.

The cameras flashed, the glare enough to make Elijah blink.

Porter hurried them both down from the platform so that the fighters at the top of the bill could take their turn. He put his hand on Connolly's shoulder and started to berate him; Elijah couldn't hear what he said, and quickly moved away as the press called out to the remaining fighters for their thoughts on the upcoming bout and what they were going to do to each other.

HE SAW her waiting at the edge of the room. She was older than him—Elijah guessed twenty-five or twenty-six—and stunning. She was tall and slender, with prominent cheekbones and long black hair that glistened in the artificial light. She was looking at him, too, and, as he made his way to the exit, she moved to intercept him. Elijah found that his mouth was dry as she drew closer, a smile on her face that exposed perfectly white teeth.

"Hello," she said.

"Hello."

"That was brilliant," she said.

"Thanks," he said, feeling the heat in his cheeks.

"You got in his head."

"You think?"

"He couldn't even look you in the eye," she said. "Yeah, you're in his head."

"He's good," he said, surprising himself at the need to defend his opponent.

"I know he is," she said. "You're better. What round?"

"Sorry?"

"What round are you going to knock him out?"

He found himself smiling at her. "My trainer says he won't go down easy," he said. "He's never been stopped before."

"What do you think?"

"Second round." He grinned.

"Is that worth a bet?"

"Take it to the bank," he said, his confidence returning.

"I'm Alesha."

"Mustafa," he said, only just remembering that he couldn't introduce himself as Elijah.

She put a hand on his arm and nodded her head. "I think someone wants you."

Elijah looked to the exit and saw McCauley waiting for him there. *Shit.*

"I'm sorry," he said. "That's my trainer. He says he has to keep me on a tight leash."

"Does that mean you can't go out and get dinner?"

"Sorry?"

"I should've said—I'm a journalist. I write for Vice. My editor sent me down here to report on Yankovich and

Cullum, but I'm much more interested in you." She smiled and reached out with her hand to touch his arm. "I was wondering, if it's okay with you and him"—she gestured over to McCauley—"maybe we could get something to eat? I could interview you. Is that possible before a fight?"

Elijah's brain seemed to be stuck in neutral: it was the smile she had given him. She wasn't just asking him out for an interview, even though that, alone, would have been flattering enough. She was asking him out. He couldn't believe that someone as gorgeous as she was—older than him, more sophisticated—could be interested in him.

"You don't *have* to," she said.

"No," Elijah said. "We could go to Nando's or something?"

She took out her phone. "What's your number?"

Elijah gave it to her and watched as she tapped it onto the keypad.

"There," she said as Elijah's phone buzzed in his pocket. "You've got mine now, too. Give me a call when you know if you're free. I'm not doing anything the night after tomorrow." She leaned in, put her hand on his shoulder and kissed his cheek. "Good luck," she said, her lips brushing his ear.

"Thanks." He swallowed, backing away and bumping into one of the photographers, who was just in the process of putting away his tripod. The equipment clattered to the floor. "Sorry," Elijah said, stepping to the side. Then, with a bashful smile at the girl, he made his way to where McCauley was waiting for him.

"Who was that?" he asked.

"Journalist."

"What did she want?"

"What do you think? Wants to interview me."

McCauley put his hand on Elijah's shoulder and guided him into the hotel lobby. Some of the other fighters were there, mixing with their entourages, some of them speaking to the press and the fans who had come to watch the conference.

"You're a great fighter, Mustafa, but you're naïve."

"No, I ain't!"

"You're going to get a lot of attention now. Girls are going to want to get to know you—you're going to have to be careful."

"She's a *journalist*."

"That's it? Nothing else? I saw how she was stroking your arm."

"You think?"

McCauley rolled his eyes. "Some of them will just want a bit of the action. They'll think that getting to know you will mean they'll be on their way to the big time. They'll want you to think that they like you—some will, but most of them won't. You'll be a means to an end. It won't just be women, either. Promoters. Other trainers who'll say they can do a better job than me."

Elijah put his arm around the older man. "Don't be a dick," he said. "I'm not trading you in."

McCauley removed Elijah's arm and gently moved him into a quieter antechamber. "I know that," he said. "And I don't want to lecture you, either, but I've been here before. If you win, things are going to go up a notch. If you win a belt, it'll get crazy. Not everyone can handle it. The temptation. Women. Money. Parties. The great ones know that they need to dedicate themselves to their sport. Those who don't... Well," he went on, "you don't hear anything else about those ones."

"Buzzkill..."

"*Mustafa.*" He sighed.

"I'm kidding," Elijah said. "I know. I'll be careful. And I'll always listen to your advice."

"No, you won't," McCauley said wryly.

"Fine—but can I buy her dinner?"

McCauley reached out and squeezed his arm. "She's a good-looking woman," he said. "Would you listen if I said no?"

"Probably not."

"Then you don't need my blessing, do you?"

Elijah grinned at McCauley. They had worked together for years, and now he knew him too well.

"Come on," McCauley said. "Let's go and get something to eat."

PART VII

THE SIXTH DAY

19

Milton rose early and went for another run in Victoria Park. He pushed himself hard, feeling the jackhammer beat of his heart and feeling the bracing sting of the cold air in his lungs. He was dripping with sweat as he slowly jogged back to the hotel, and drew a slightly disapproving look from the smartly dressed woman who stepped out of the lift as he waited to descend. There was a pool in the basement; Milton showered off the sweat, changed into a pair of swimming trunks, stepped into the warm atrium in which the pool had been built, and lowered himself into the water. He swam for thirty minutes, five strokes for every lap, and then took a sauna to ease his muscles. He showered and went back to his room.

He took out his phone and checked for messages. Ziggy had sent Milton a link to a web page that he had built, together with an explanation of what he had done that Milton did not entirely understand. It appeared that he had taken the tools that Google made available for developers who wanted to work with their map products and then had incorporated the tracking data that he had purloined from the phones registered to Sharon and Elijah Warriner. The result was a dynamically updated map that showed where both phones were at all times. Milton opened the link on his own phone and checked to see where they both were: Elijah was on Hampstead Heath and, judging by the route that he followed and the steady updating of the phone's location, he had gone out for a run; Sharon was nearer by, in London Fields.

That was convenient. Milton wasn't sure how Elijah would react to seeing him again. He would test the ground with his mother first.

It was a mile to London Fields. Milton grabbed a bagel from the breakfast bar and ate it on the way, heading north along Mare Street. Tired Christmas decorations were hanging from lampposts, and a few of the shops had made the effort to brighten up their displays for the festive season.

Milton checked Ziggy's map; Sharon was near the lido on the northwest side of the park. He set out, sharing the path with mothers pushing their babies in prams, joggers pounding the pavement, and dog owners exercising their pets. No one paid him any mind; everyone else was busy with their own lives, and he looked like just another pedestrian out for a morning walk.

He saw her sitting on a bench inside the railings that marked the boundary of the lido. She had a Styrofoam cup of coffee on the table in front of her and was warming her hands around it. She was wearing a headscarf that obscured most of her head and face, a thick coat and jeans, but her hands were unclothed; he was still a distance away, but he thought he could see white streaks across the black skin.

Milton took a deep breath. Sharon had been badly burned after her flat had been torched. Milton had gone in to get her out, and remembered it as if it were yesterday: how he had wrapped his coat around his hand so that he could touch the red-hot handle, the hungry roar of the fire as it consumed everything, the panic on the faces of the neighbours, the screams that he had heard from inside. He had gone into the blaze and brought her out. He remembered the aftermath too well: her body wrapped in bandages, the stubble on her head from where her hair had been burned off, the puckered skin on her face and body, and the wheeze of her breathing through the tube that had been fitted into her mouth. Rutherford had brought Elijah to the hospital; Milton had made him promise to look after the boy as he had left to exact vengeance for the unforgivable escalation of the violence by Bizness and his crew.

He had done that, but his anger had blinded him to the threat that Control still posed. Twelve had found him, and Rutherford had died because Milton had allowed himself to be distracted.

He took a breath, trying to put the memory aside. He went through the gates and stopped next to the table.

"Hello, Sharon."

She looked up at him and, for a moment, he thought that she wouldn't recognise him.

"John?" she said.

She got up from the table, knocking over the cup of coffee in her haste. She ignored it, stepping closer and throwing her arms around him. Milton held her tight, and they stayed like that for a long moment.

Milton gently disengaged himself from her embrace. "It's been a long time."

"I thought..." she began, then stopped. The joy in her

face flickered a little and then was occluded by doubt. “Where did you go? You just disappeared.”

Milton looked down at the pool of coffee that had spilled over the table. “Do you want another one?” he said. “There’s quite a lot to tell you.”

20

Sharon had mopped up the spilt coffee with a hunk of napkins. Milton put the two fresh coffees on the table and sat down opposite her. He sipped one, taking the opportunity to look at her more carefully. Her hair had grown back and she wore it long, no doubt to obscure the burns to her neck and shoulders. The doctors had told him that they would be able to graft skin onto her face and it looked as if they had done just that; it looked different, lighter than perhaps it should have, but it was an improvement on what he remembered. Some areas had been repaired better than others. The skin on her throat looked rougher than it should, a slightly different shade to the skin that he could see in the space above her loosely knotted scarf.

"How have you been?" he asked her, delaying the more difficult conversation that he knew he would have to initiate.

"I'm good," she said.

"You look good."

"You don't need to say that."

"I'm serious."

She pointed to her face. "Six different grafts," she said. "But there's only so much they can do." She held out her hands; they were scarred, with raised lesions that looked as if they were still healing, even all this time later. "The rest of my body still looks like that. It won't get much better."

He started to speak, then stopped; he didn't know what to say.

"I'm fine, John," she said. "And if it wasn't for you, I wouldn't be here at all."

Milton returned her smile. She was absolving him, but he found it hard to agree. Grandiosity was one of the things that they warned you to look out for in Alcoholics Anonymous. He had heard it in one of the first meetings he had attended: drunks were apt to look down on everyone else even when they were lying in the gutter. He had assumed that he could insert himself into the lives of Sharon and Elijah, saving the boy from a wasted life on the streets. It had been arrogance on his part, and it hadn't turned out like that, at least not at first; Sharon had nearly been killed, and the boy's life had been turned upside down.

"Where have you been?" she asked him.

"Here and there."

"Where are you living?"

"I don't really have a place I'd say was home. I've been in Tenerife."

"You're travelling?"

"You could call it that."

"And now?"

"I saw Elijah on TV—one of his fights. It was amazing. I couldn't believe how far he'd come, and then I saw he had the fight on Christmas Eve. It's safe for me to be here now—I thought I'd get a ticket and come to watch."

"*Safe?* What do you mean?"

"That's a long story."

"You've had three years to tell it."

Milton paused, still not quite sure how he would broach the matter of his history. "Did the police speak to you?"

"Of course," she said. "You know Elijah found Rutherford's body?"

"Oh, shit." Milton groaned. "I'm sorry."

"It's not me you want to say sorry to," she said. "It's him. He blamed you. I think he still does."

"I'd blame me, too."

"They think you shot him."

"I didn't."

"I believe you," she replied, immediately and with conviction. "I told the police that, too. Have you ever spoken to them about it?"

"No," he said. "And I'd rather not."

She let that go. "So what happened?"

"There's a lot about me that I didn't tell you," he said.

"I guessed that."

"And there's a lot I still can't say." He paused and looked out over the park. "I used to work for the government. I can't say what I did, but it wasn't pleasant. I decided that I'd had enough, and I wanted to leave. The problem I had was that my job wasn't one that was easy to walk away from. You can't just resign. The man I worked for was unhappy with my decision—let's leave it at that."

He stopped again, allowing himself to remember. He had been living with Rutherford while Sharon had recovered in the hospital. Elijah was staying in a room next to his mother, and, as she improved and moved from the burns unit to a general ward, he had been about to move in with Rutherford, too. Milton would have moved on at that point, but events had intervened.

"It was a week after the fire. You were in the hospital. Rutherford had arranged a fight night with another gym in Tottenham."

"Elijah told me," she said. "He won."

"He did," Milton said. "I was there. He looked good. Rutherford said that we should all go back to his house for a takeaway. I was fixing the wiring at the gym and I wanted to get it done. I said I'd come over later."

"But you didn't."

"No. The man I used to work for sent another man to kill me. He had a gun on me when Rutherford came back. Rutherford wasn't supposed to be there. The man shot Rutherford. The distraction was enough to give me a chance. He shot me in the shoulder, but I managed to get the gun from him."

"The police didn't say there was anyone else there—just Rutherford's body."

"He wouldn't have waited for the police."

Milton thought of Twelve. Milton had put a bullet in his knee so that he could get away, but the man had kept on coming. He had reappeared in Juárez and then in Russia, Control's faithful bloodhound to the end.

"And you?"

"I was hurt," Milton said. "I knew that they would send others after me, so I did the only thing that I could. I left the country."

"You could've gone to the police."

Milton shook his head. "They wouldn't have believed me, and it wouldn't have mattered. The people I worked for would have known where I was, and they would have been able to get to me. But that wasn't what I was worried about. They would have been able to get to you, too—you and Elijah. Bad things happen to people who get too close to me.

Rutherford was shot. You were hurt. I couldn't bear the thought of anything else happening, so I ran."

She looked at him silently and then reached a hand across the table and covered his with it. "That explains a lot."

"Really?"

She nodded. "A man and a woman came to talk to Elijah afterwards. Not police—this was after they had finished. They were asking about you. They told him that you were dangerous and that they needed to find you. They talked to me, too, said the same things. I told them I didn't know where you were. I *didn't* know—it wasn't a lie. I told Elijah not to believe the things that they said."

"And?"

"I don't know," she admitted. "I don't know what he thinks."

They watched as a class of young schoolchildren passed into the lido, chattering happily among themselves.

"What happened afterwards?" Milton asked.

"I was in the hospital for two months," she said. "Elijah was with me some of the time, but he had to go to school, too. I couldn't keep an eye on him. I know how close Elijah was to falling in with the wrong crowd. You got him out of it, but I knew it wouldn't matter if we stayed where we were. You know another boy was shot that week—in Victoria Park?"

Milton nodded. The boy—Pops—had been murdered for disobeying Bizness.

"Elijah said he knew him. And then he said one of the boys who he used to hang around with—Shaquille, his name is, but they all call him Pinky—Elijah said that he threatened him, said he had a gun and he was going to shoot him. I called the police, and the boy was arrested.

Elijah said I shouldn't have done it, and maybe I shouldn't have. The boy got out, and Elijah said he was scared. There was no way we could stay. My cousin lives in Margate. I sent Elijah to stay with her, and then I went too when I was well enough to come out again. He started boxing properly; it went well, and we moved to Sheffield when they said he should train with the national team. I found a place for us up there, near the gym where Elijah works out. It's nothing like it is down here. No one knows us. Even now that Elijah is doing well, no one knows who we are. It's nice."

"So why are you back?"

"The fight," she said. "He's training today, and I had some time to kill. I thought I'd come over and see the old place. I haven't been back since we left."

"You think it's changed?"

"Some of it has," she said. She gestured to the lido and then the well-heeled mothers who were pushing expensive prams around the park. "There's more money here than there was. Houses are more expensive. But some of it—not so much."

She frowned, her expression darkening with worry. Milton could see that Sharon still had concerns; he was about to ask her what was the matter when she checked her watch, swore under her breath, and got up.

"I've got to go," she said. "I'm seeing Elijah."

Milton stood, too. "It's good to see you."

She hugged him again. "What are you doing tomorrow?"

"Nothing planned."

"Do you want to have lunch with me?"

"I'd like that very much."

"Do you know Victoria Park? There's a café near the boating lake—do you want to meet there?"

He said that he knew it, and they settled on a time. They

walked to the gate; Sharon was going to get a bus on Richmond Road, and Milton decided that he would walk back to the hotel.

"Good seeing you, John," she said.

"And you." He paused. "Do you think he'd see me? Elijah?"

She sighed. "I don't know," she said. "He's been angry about what happened for years, and I'm not sure that I want to distract him with it now, before the fight."

"No," Milton said. "You're right. That's the last thing we want to do. Forget I said it."

"He was very fond of you, John. That's why he took it so badly. Let me have a think about it."

PART VIII

THE FIFTH DAY

21

Milton got up at five again, went out running for an hour, and then exercised in the hotel gym. He went back to his room to see a missed call from Ziggy. He called him back.

"What are you doing?" Ziggy said without preamble.

"Good morning to you, too."

"I'm outside."

Milton frowned. "I didn't tell you where I was staying."

"Come on, Milton," Ziggy said, sighing theatrically. "You used your credit card to check in."

"You know my credit card?"

"You'd be surprised what I know."

"Actually," Milton countered, "I wouldn't. But I'm not going to ask. Where are you?"

"There's a café across the road. I've gone through the phone you gave me. I thought you might want me to take you through it. You can buy me breakfast to say thanks."

~

Ziggy was waiting for him in Hulya's Café Restaurant, a greasy spoon a little way down the road from the hotel. Milton crossed and went inside, taking off his coat. Ziggy had a table in the front of the room and was nursing a coffee in a chipped mug. The proprietor had made an effort to decorate the café for Christmas, with an artificial tree on the counter and threadbare tinsel strung out over the illuminated board that displayed the menu.

"What do you want?" Milton said, nodding back to the counter.

"Full English," he said, grinning. He finished his coffee. "And another one, please."

"You'd better have something good for me," Milton said, playing along.

"You won't be disappointed."

Milton went to the counter and ordered two full English breakfasts with two coffees. The proprietor took his money, scooped instant coffee into two mugs, and then filled them with hot water from an urn that leaked a cloud of steam. He handed over the mugs and said that he would bring over the two breakfasts.

Milton took the coffees to the table and sat down.

"So," Ziggy said. "Have you met your friend?"

"His mother," Milton said.

"I did a little more research on the two of them," Ziggy said. "They used to live near here, didn't they?"

Milton nodded as he sipped at his coffee.

"I found some old newspaper stories about the boy. He found the body of a local man in a gym three years ago. Your name was mentioned—said the police wanted to speak to you."

"I was in the process of trying to leave the Group," Milton said, speaking quietly so that the man at the only other occupied table wouldn't be able to overhear him. "Control sent Twelve to take me out."

"The local man?"

"Wrong place, wrong time."

The proprietor delivered their breakfasts: sausages, eggs, bacon, cooked tomatoes, beans and fried bread. Milton thanked him and waited until he went back to the counter before speaking again.

"There's no point talking about that now. What did you get?"

Ziggy sliced one of the sausages into three and slotted a segment into his mouth. "I downloaded everything off the phone and everything he was storing in the cloud," he said as he chewed. "I've got an algorithm running through his photos and videos now, sorting them so I can filter through them more efficiently. I'll tell you if anything pops out at me."

"Email?"

"Kids don't email, grandad. It's mostly social media and messaging apps."

"Go on, then."

"I got quite a bit. Basics first. The phone is registered to an Edwin Ogunsola. He bought it from the Carphone Warehouse in Kingsland Shopping Centre. The contract is registered to 15 Greenwood Road in Dalston, and he's paying for it with a Lloyds debit card. I looked at his account—frequent cash deposits, balance of a touch over £6000. Not bad for a nineteen-year-old who doesn't appear to have a job."

Milton stabbed his fork into a piece of the fried bread, dipped it in the beans and ate it.

"I looked through the call history, and there are four numbers he calls more than any others. His mother, first of all. After that, he calls numbers registered to Rowmando Silcott, Tyrone Godwin and Shaquille Abora. They're listed in his phonebook as Kidz, Chips and Pinky. You know any of them?"

"I've heard the names," Milton said.

"No voicemails apart from his mum. I looked at the phone's location data—that was more useful. Apart from his home address, the place that comes up most often is a terraced house on Langford Close. I ran a check on the police national database—officers have been called out there five times in the last six months. Complaints from the neighbours mostly, but the anti-drugs team think it's being used as a crack house."

Milton nodded and wondered whether he might need to pay a visit to the address. "This is good, Ziggy," he said, knowing from long experience that Ziggy was insecure and worked best when his ego was flattered.

"I'm not finished," he said. "I was able to get into all his social accounts. I've pulled the last week's worth of updates and private messages and put them into a Dropbox folder. I'll email you the link. There's a gig's worth of data for you to look through—some light reading for later. They message each other most often on Telegram, probably because the encryption is tough to crack. Not hard at all if you have the phone they use, of course. I've dumped the recent messages into the folder, but I thought you might want to see this straight away."

Ziggy turned the screen around so that Milton could read it.

PINKY >> The little pussy is on our turf tomorrow.

KIDZ >> What you wanna do?

PINKY >> What you think? He's gonna get smoked.

CHIPS >> You told Sol?

PINKY >> Don't worry about Sol.

Milton skimmed the rest of the exchange. It was mostly boasting and showing off, with Pinky telling the others that the 'pussy'—Milton took that to be Elijah—was going to be working out at York Hall, that it was open to the public, and that they should go down and let him know that he was going to get 'merked.'

"Great." Milton sighed.

"Trouble?"

"Always. Do you know who Sol is?"

Ziggy shook his head. "A couple of other references to him, but no phone number or much of anything else."

"Keep looking."

"There's one thing we could do," he said. "We can send a location-sharing request to all three of them. If they accept it, we'll be able to track where they are."

Milton thought about that. "But if they know that this phone was taken?"

"Then they'll know someone is looking into them."

"Do it."

"All right," Ziggy said. He took Little Mark's phone, and his fingers flashed across the screen. "Done."

Milton took the phone and put it into his pocket. He stood up. "Thanks, Ziggy."

"Let me know if you need anything else," he said.

"I will."

22

Milton took his time as he made his way to the café where he had agreed to meet Sharon. He headed east, walked up Approach Road, and passed between the tall stone gates into the park. Joggers and cyclists passed him in both directions as he strolled along the path; he was early, so he sat down on a bench and watched the swans and ducks that had gathered around the Chinese pagoda that was a rather incongruous addition to the island in the middle of the lake.

He wondered what Sharon would say to him. It was obvious that something had been on her mind when they had spoken yesterday, and he didn't know whether she would want to raise it. He determined that he wouldn't push her to talk if she didn't want to; he was there to help if she asked, but he was less arrogant now than he had been before, less certain that his intervention in her life could bring only good things. He wondered about Elijah, too, and whether she had told the boy that he was back. Milton had a ticket to the fight and hoped that he would be able to see it, at least; he would have liked to have the chance to speak to

Elijah, but that was out of his hands. There was no sense in worrying about something that he could not control.

The Pavilion Café was on the edge of the water. It was a small, domed building with seating inside and out. A platform reached out a short distance over the water and allowed additional tables with pleasing views. Milton went inside. It was busy, but the staff were administering the lengthy queue with good humour. Milton saw Sharon sitting in a corner and made his way across the room to her.

"Hello again," she said.

"How are you?"

"I'm good. Thanks for coming. I got you a coffee—I hope that's all right?"

"Perfect," he said, sitting down in the seat opposite hers.

He sipped the drink and looked across the table at Sharon. She had taken off her heavy coat and slung it across the back of the chair. He could see the burns on her neck now, running up to her ears on both sides of her head. She was wearing an open shirt, and she had rolled up her sleeves so that Milton could see the scars on her arms, too. She wasn't ashamed of them; to the contrary, it appeared that she barely gave them a moment's thought. She was an impressive woman; Milton had always thought that and was reminded of it now.

"How's everything else?" Milton asked her.

"What do you mean? Family?"

Milton nodded.

"My husband is still in prison. There was talk of him getting out, but something happened inside—some fight or something like that—and his sentence was increased. He's got another five years to serve."

"Has he ever been in touch?"

"As soon as he found out that Elijah was doing well."

She laughed bitterly. "He started sending birthday cards and letters. He was trying to get Elijah to go and visit him, but he's not interested. He's never been in Elijah's life and Elijah is *smart*. He knows exactly why he's got in touch again. No." She shook her head. "He's wasting his time."

"What about your other son? I'm sorry—I can't remember his name."

"Jules?" she said. "I'm afraid he's not with us anymore."

"I'm sorry..." Milton began.

"Don't," she said. "It was sad, but it was inevitable. He wasn't interested in getting well."

"What happened?"

"He overdosed," she said matter-of-factly. "They found him near Waterloo station. It's been a couple of years now. Elijah was angry for the first few months, but he's been able to deal with it, just like I did. It's just me and him now."

Milton sipped his coffee and waited as Sharon did the same.

"There was something I've been meaning to ask you," Milton said.

"I think I can probably guess," she said. "Why did we change our names?"

"Yes," he said, laughing.

"It's a long story. There was a mosque when we were down in Margate. We started going to it, must have been a month or two after Jules died. We were both looking for something, I suppose, and I had a friend who went there. Elijah came home one day and said that his name had a bad meaning, that he had taken *shahada*, and that was that. He was Mustafa. I changed my name, too."

"Adara?"

"Yes," she said. "How do you know that?"

"I've got a friend who's very good at finding things out," he said.

Sharon smiled at something. "He kept it up for a month, and then he said he didn't mind if I called him Elijah again."

"Is he still religious?"

She shrugged. "Not really. More spiritual, perhaps. He says it's helped him. I think it did. He's calmer, at least most of the time."

"What about you?"

"Religion?" She laughed sadly. "I don't know why I thought it would help me—I've seen too much in my life to have any time for that. I changed my name for practical reasons. I thought it would make it more difficult to find us if anyone started to look."

They drank their coffees quietly for a moment. Milton looked out onto the boating lake as a swan splashed down onto the glassy surface.

"Did you see Elijah yesterday?" Milton asked.

"Briefly. He looks ready. I said he must be nervous, but he said he wasn't. He knows how good he is; that's the problem."

"How do you mean?"

"His trainer says his only weakness is arrogance. Elijah says it's not arrogance if he backs it up." She smiled and shook her head. "He's always been like that, even back when you knew him. He's shy, underneath it all, but he won't ever let you see that. It's all about attitude, what he wants you to think. He says that's why he's good at boxing—he doesn't let them see he's scared."

"Did you mention that you'd seen me?"

"I didn't have time," she said. "I will. But there is a place you might be able to see him."

"Where?"

"He's got a public workout tomorrow at York Hall. Do you know it?"

Milton said that he did.

She reached into her handbag and took out an embossed pass that hung from a lanyard. "It's at midday. This'll get you through security."

Milton took it, turned it over and looked at it. 'Muhammad v Connolly' was written across it in bold type and, beneath that, PRESS. He put it in his pocket.

"Thanks," he said.

She frowned, just like she had yesterday.

"What is it?" he asked her.

"Nothing."

"It's not nothing. Something's worrying you."

She sighed. "I was over at the estate before I saw you yesterday. I still have a couple of friends there, girls who had kids the same time I did. They all know about Elijah now. I knew it was coming, but it seemed to take forever. Every time he was on the television, I was sure someone would see him. His new name helped, I suppose; people could read about him in the papers without realising it was him. And he's bigger now—he looks different from when he was fifteen. All those other fights were small, and if they got on the TV, it was late at night when the only people who'd be watching were real fans, people who loved boxing, not random people who live down on the estate. But he's second on the bill for this fight. They're making all these predictions about what'll happen if he wins, how much money he might make, all that. There's a lot of hype."

"That's the business," Milton said.

"I know. But it worries me."

"You think some of the boys he used to hang out with might find out?"

"They *will* find out," she said. "They probably already have. I'm worried about what they might try to do. Well, one of them, anyway—Pinky. You probably didn't meet him when you were here, but there was always something about him that frightened me. His eyes—there was nothing there. Lifeless, like he had no soul."

"I remember him," he said.

Milton considered his own role in what had happened and knew that he wouldn't be able to walk away. He remembered the kids in the gang from before. They had been young boys then, but that was three years ago. Elijah had grown into a man; they would have, too. They would see one of their own doing well, and it would grate on them that they hadn't had the same good fortune. He wasn't about to say it to Sharon, but he agreed with her: she was right to be nervous.

"It doesn't matter," she said with a wave of a hand. "It's just me worrying about nothing. We've never had much luck before. Everything's going so well now; part of me says we don't deserve it and it's all going to come crashing down."

"It's not," Milton said. "You deserve to be happy."

Sharon's eyes were filmy and her lip quivered. Milton was reminded of the things that kept him awake at night. He was always going to be behind on the ledger of good against bad. He thought about the ninth step and the atonement that he would never be able to make. He had too much ground to make up, but that wouldn't stop him from trying.

"Look," Milton said, placing his hands on the table palm down. "I'm going to make myself useful while I'm here."

"You don't have to—"

Milton laid his hand on hers and gently interrupted her. "I'll be there tomorrow. I won't let anything happen to him."

23

There was a branch of Nando's just a short walk from Bethnal Green station. The road was busy here, with businesses on either side and the stalls from the market set up next to the kerbs. It was six and darkness had fallen two hours ago; the stalls were lit by artificial lights that had been fitted above, cables trailing to small portable generators that chugged away in the background. The trading day was drawing to a close, and the stallholders were trying to offload whatever they had left, calling out knock-down prices in an attempt to attract those passers-by who might be tempted by a bargain. There was a pub opposite the restaurant—The Star of Bethnal Green—and a sign in the window suggested it was suitable for GROWN-UP RAVERS and BOOZERS OF CHOICE. Hipster irony, Elijah thought. It was everywhere.

He was there early and, as he waited, he wondered whether he should have suggested somewhere else. The restaurant was busy, the clientele young and noisy. Alesha was a good five years older than he was, and, he thought, more sophisticated than this. He didn't know anything about clothes and make-up, but even he could tell that the stuff she had been wearing at the press conference was expensive. He wanted to impress her, and he realised, with a dose of embarrassment, that his suggestion might not deliver the right impression. Elijah looked across the road to the pub; he wondered if he had time to stop in for a shot of Dutch courage.

But he didn't; he turned and saw her making her way along the pavement from the direction of the station.

"Hello," she said. "Sorry I'm late."

"You're not," he said, hurrying to absolve her.

"I am. Ten minutes. The trains."

"I only just got here," he said.

"You're too kind." She stepped in closer, put her hand on his shoulder, and kissed him lightly on the cheek. "I'm pleased we could do this. I thought—you know, with the fight and everything..."

"I can still go out for dinner," he said.

"Can you have a drink?"

"Course," he said.

"I was thinking we could go over there first," she said, nodding over the road to the pub. "I wouldn't mind a glass of mulled wine before we eat."

THEY FOUND a table at the front of the pub's main room. Alesha took off her coat and draped it over the back of the chair. She was wearing leather trousers, a denim shirt and a chunky cable-knit sweater.

"What do you want?" she asked him.

"No," he said, raising a hand. "I'll get them."

"You can get the next round."

"You don't want to eat?"

"No rush. What do you want?"

"Orange juice," he said sheepishly.

"Sure?"

He thought of McCauley; he wouldn't be impressed if he drank alcohol before the fight. "I'd better not."

"Look after the table," she said, taking her purse and making her way to the bar.

He sat down and watched as Alesha placed her order. She was *fine*: tall and slender, dressed better than the other girls in the pub, and with an air about her that Elijah found both intimidating and attractive. He still felt weird that she would want to spend time with him, even though he knew, from what McCauley had said, that he could expect more attention as he became better known. That was fine in theory, but it was still difficult to wrap his head around it. He was just a kid from around these ends, a hood rat who had never been much good at school, had never had the confidence to talk to girls, only given a chance to be someone because he could fight.

Alesha came back with the drinks: an orange juice for Elijah and a large glass of mulled wine for her. She put the glasses on the table and sat down. Her right wrist was heavy with an assortment of colourful bracelets that rattled as she took her drink and held it up for a toast.

"Good luck for the fight," she said. "Not that I think you'll need it."

Elijah took his orange juice and self-consciously touched it against her glass. He drank; she was looking at him with a mischievous smile.

"Vodka and orange?" he said, looking at the drink.

"Might have slipped a shot in there. That all right?"

Elijah couldn't help but laugh. "If my trainer finds out..."

"I'm not going to tell him," she said.

He put the glass to his lips again and took another sip. He watched her as she sipped at her wine, then put her glass down on the table and ran her fingers through her hair.

She put her elbows on the table and rested her chin on her laced fingers. "Are you worried?"

"About the fight?"

She nodded.

"Nah," he said. "Not really. The training's gone well."

"But Connolly's good."

"So am I." He grinned, pleased to find a little of his usual pep.

"I know you are," she replied. "I've watched all your fights on YouTube."

"You have?"

"I told you," she said, "I'm going to write a piece on you. I'm doing my research."

"What was your favourite?"

"The Adichie fight, I think. Everyone was saying how good he was. Didn't look like anyone took you seriously."

"They did after I knocked him out," he said.

She beamed at him, raised her glass and toasted him again. He felt relaxed in her company. She was easy to talk to, and it was difficult not to be flattered by the attention that she was giving him.

"Who do you write for?" he asked. "I know you said, but I can't remember."

"Vice."

"What's that—online?"

She sipped her wine and nodded. "And TV."

"And why do you want to write about me?"

"Why?" she said, smiling at him. "Seriously? Because you're going to be famous. I want to get to know you before that happens—you won't talk to people like me after that."

"What are you talking about?"

"You won't be coming out to places like this for much longer. It'll be Mayfair. Private jets. Magnums of champagne."

"Nah," he said, unable to stifle his grin. "I ain't gonna change."

"That's what they all say."

He took his drink and sipped it. He couldn't believe how well this was going. Alesha had a way about her, a naturalness that lent him a sense of ease and confidence. He was enjoying himself in her company.

She put her glass down on the table, reached down into her bag, and took out a notepad and a pen. "Go on, then," she said. "What's your story?"

"What do you want to know?"

"Your background. You're not from Sheffield, are you?"

"No," he said. "I grew up in London—not far from here. Hackney."

"So why'd you leave?"

"Lots of reasons," he said.

He glanced down at Alesha's notepad and remembered that he was on the record. He wondered how much he should say, and decided that he would prefer to keep things a little vague. He hadn't anticipated being asked about his background, and hadn't given thought to how much he would be comfortable having out there. He had nothing to hide about his upbringing. He had done some things that he wasn't proud of, but that was a long time ago, and he had grown up a lot since then. But things had happened when he was sixteen that had frightened him, and he didn't want to revisit them: the murders of Pops and Rutherford were uppermost in his mind, and the altercation with Pinky that had precipitated their move to Margate.

"You're very mysterious," she said.

"Not really."

"What about Islam?" she said.

He shuffled a little in his seat. "What about it?"

"Did you convert?"

"Three years ago."

"And you changed your name?"

He nodded, but she didn't press, waiting for him to decide whether or not to elaborate. He looked across the table at her and felt bad for bringing her here and then telling her nothing.

"My name was Elijah," he said. "It still is, really—that's what my mum calls me. I'm not a very good Muslim." He hesitated. "Don't put that in the article."

She made a gesture as if to zip her lips. "Not a word."

"I had some troubles as a younger," he said, treading carefully. "Religion seemed like a good way to deal with them, at least back then."

"And now?"

"I got boxing," he said, shrugging. "Boxing is everything —it made me what I am."

"And it's not finished with you yet," she said.

Elijah noticed that she had finished her drink. He drained the rest of his vodka and orange and stood. "You want another?"

"Go on then."

THEY DIDN'T GO to the restaurant. They stayed in the pub until eleven, then took an Uber to get bagels from the twenty-four-hour deli on Brick Lane. Alesha had a flat ten minutes away, just outside Spitalfields, and Elijah offered to walk her home. They had just set off when she slipped her hand into his and squeezed it. Her skin was warm and smooth; it felt good. Elijah was happy. The night had gone better than he could have expected. He had been careful with the drink, ordering orange juices for himself and accepting her vodkas when she bought the rounds. He had paced his intake well, and now he had a mild buzz while remaining confident that he wouldn't suffer from a hangover tomorrow.

They reached Alesha's building and paused outside it.

She looked at him. "You want to come in?"

Elijah knew that he should say no. She was so beautiful: skin like silk, a body to die for, eyes that held him and wouldn't let him go. But he knew that McCauley would disapprove, and it was late.

"I can't," he said. "I need to get back to the hotel."

She took his hand and squeezed it. "That's fine."

"It's not that I wouldn't like to..."

"I know. You've got the fight. Really, Elijah—it's fine."

He felt the heat in his cheeks. "There's a party after the fight," he said. "They say it's gonna be good. You want to come?"

"*If* you win."

"I'm going to win," he said, flashing her his teeth.

"Kidding," she said. "I know you are. Where is it?"

"I can't remember. I could text you? I think I can get you a VIP pass for the fight. That'll get you into the party, too."

"I'd love to," she said and, before he could say anything else, she leaned closer and kissed him softly on the mouth. He could taste the wine on her lips.

He felt weak and was about to change his mind. "I—"

"Good luck," she said, interrupting him. "I'll see you at the fight."

She crossed the pavement and went into the lobby, turning to give him a wave. He waited a moment, cursing himself for doing what he knew was the responsible thing, and then turned and made his way back to the main road. Big day tomorrow. He needed to get to his bed.

PART IX

THE FOURTH DAY

24

Milton found that he was nervous as he showered after his morning run. Elijah's workout was today, and Milton had no idea how he would react. Sharon had warned him that this might not be the friendly reunion that Milton would have liked; Elijah was headstrong, he always had been, and Milton knew that there was a chance that he would react badly after the way he had left things before. There was no prospect of him not going, though. He wanted to see the boy, and he was concerned about the message that Ziggy had excavated from the phone Milton had taken from Little Mark. It seemed as if the other members of the gang were going to be there, too, and Milton knew that there would be the potential for trouble. Sharon was worried about it. Milton was worried, too.

He was determined to insulate Elijah from it.

He dressed in a clean pair of jeans, a black T-shirt and his leather jacket, then pulled on his boots and laced them up. He took the press pass that Sharon had given him and slipped it over his head, zipping up the jacket and making his way outside.

It was less than a five-minute walk from his hotel to the venue. He walked by the café where he had met Ziggy yesterday, continuing by the Museum of Childhood, a large brick building that was set back from the road behind a neatly painted iron fence. York Hall was a curious building located on an estate owned by the council. The building on the main road behind which it sheltered was an ugly seventies construction, with a laundromat on the ground floor and then five storeys of council flats above it, the windows covered by dirty net curtains. Milton turned left onto the Old Ford Road and saw the Hall. It was a large brick and concrete building with lettering spelling out TOWER HAMLETS and then YORK HALL. It had originally been a Turkish bath, but it had been a boxing venue since the twenties.

Milton had never visited it before, and he felt a buzz of anticipation as he approached the queue waiting to get inside. He hung back for a moment, scanning the crowd to see if he recognised anyone. The people in the queue ranged in age and ethnicity, but it was predominantly young and black. Kids and young men, wanting to see the fighters close up, hoping to catch a glimpse of future stars, perhaps hoping that the glamour would rub off onto them.

Ziggy had provided a folder of images that he thought corresponded with Pinky, Little Mark, Kidz and Chips, and Milton had studied them. He was confident that he would have recognised them. He looked for the four of them, but they weren't there. He checked his watch: there was still twenty minutes to go before the proceedings would begin. Perhaps they wouldn't come after all. Or perhaps they would wait until everyone was inside. Milton was not prepared to lower his guard.

He ignored the grumbles from the queue, made his way to the security on the door, and held out his pass. The man examined it, grunted something affirmative, and stepped aside so that Milton could go through.

MILTON WENT INSIDE AND GAPED. The interior was eye-opening. It was a grand neo-Georgian space, with a warm wooden floor and a balcony halfway up the wall. His attention was immediately drawn upwards to the eight skylights that were fitted into the vaulted ceiling. The ring was in the centre of the space, lit by the shafts of light that fell down from above. Milton felt almost reverent: this was Mecca for British boxing. The greats had all fought here over the years —John Stracey, Charlie Magri, Maurice Hope, Nigel Benn— all young men with big dreams, willing to spill their blood on the canvas to make it big. Many of them had.

But, still, those had been fight nights, and this was just a public workout. The idea was a new one for Milton, but he realised that modern media was voracious for content and knew that this would sell a few more pay-per-views.

The doors were opened and the onlookers started to come inside, filling in the spaces around the ring, some of them taking seats in the balcony above. Milton worked his way through the crowd.

"Man's gonna get sparked out in the third," said one spectator. "Trust me."

"Nah," the man next to him disagreed. "Not gonna happen, blood. Mustafa's the real deal."

Milton eavesdropped on the conversations and gauged the mood. Elijah's opponent was from Tottenham, and Milton guessed that most of the crowd were here because of him. Others—the ones who spoke more knowledgeably—had come to get a glimpse of the exciting prospect from Sheffield.

Music started to play from big bass bins, and Milton looked up to see a DJ on the balcony. He circulated, as inconspicuously as possible, but very aware that a middle-aged white man wouldn't blend easily into this mostly black crowd. He found a spot at the back of the room where he could see the entrance and the ring. The fighters from lower down the card came out. Milton remembered them from the conference he had watched on his phone. They passed through the ropes one at a time, introduced by the brash young promoter who had chosen to dress as Santa in reference to the fast-approaching holiday that he had hijacked for his event. He was wearing a red suit and hat and an extravagantly long beard, and he stood back as they went through their routines. They worked out with their trainers, firing punches into pads, showing off their footwork. The sound of leather on leather echoed around the hall, a staccato accompaniment to music that Milton couldn't identify and that made him feel old.

He changed position, looking for different perspectives, searching for faces that he might recognise. Still nothing. No one stood out. A fighter stepped out of the ring and was replaced by the next one up, a cruiserweight with tattoos all over his body.

Milton moved closer to the ring, using his pass to get closer to the fighters who had finished their workouts. They were being interviewed on small cameras and mobile phones; he guessed that the footage was being broadcast on Facebook or YouTube. Milton had trawled some of the accounts that had been established to show off this kind of coverage. He had learned about this new form of boxing—a lot different to how it had been at its height when Milton was a younger man. Back then, Chris Eubank and Nigel Benn had traded barbs on TV chat shows. Now it seemed every fighter was a minor star who had 'beef' with another fighter. It had led to a resurgence in interest in the sport, but it seemed everyone with a mobile phone could now have a channel on YouTube to report on it.

Milton didn't understand that at all.

Maybe he was getting old.

25

They took an Uber from the estate to Bethnal Green. Pinky looked out of the window of the car and tried to ignore the uneasiness he felt as they passed out of their postcode and into enemy territory. The Bethnal Green Massive controlled this part of town, and Pinky knew that they would react badly if they knew that members of a rival gang were here. There had been beef between the LFB and the BGM before, and Pinky remembered a series of competing videos that had been uploaded to YouTube, each gang threatening the other in increasingly graphic terms. He wasn't afraid of confrontation, but he didn't need the distraction today. They had business to do.

"What you reckon it's going to be like?" Chips said.

"Ain't got no idea," Pinky said. "Never been to anything like this before."

"I can't get my head around JaJa," Kidz said. "Skinny little bredren; never would've said he would've come to anything."

"He did always have a punch on him," Little Mark offered, grinning. "You remember, Pinky?"

"Shut the fuck up," Pinky said, the memory still fresh. "Little pussy ain't gonna be so full of it when he sees us again. The youngers there okay?"

Chips looked at his phone. "They say they are. Inside. Ready to go."

"How many?"

"I got ten of 'em."

"Good."

The driver pulled onto the Old Ford Road and parked outside a large brick and concrete building with a small queue of young men waiting outside it. Pinky looked at the time on his phone: the workout was scheduled to have begun twenty minutes earlier. Pinky opened the door and got out, waiting for the others to join him. He led the way across the pavement and up to the end of the queue.

"You remember what we're gonna do?" he asked the others.

"Chill," Kidz said. "It ain't no thing."

Pinky clenched his fists: open and closed, open and closed. He felt the prickle of anticipation. He had unfinished business with JaJa. The little bitch had got his mum to call the police on him; that was bad enough, but it wasn't what stung the most. It was the moment in the ring when he had sparked him out. Pinky could close his eyes and still picture it, could still feel the jarring blow against his jaw, the taste of blood in his mouth. He remembered it and so did the others; Little Mark had just shown that. That was what bugged Pinky the most. The others were laughing at it, a joke at his expense, and if Little Mark was prepared to needle him in front of Kidz and Chips, what were the others saying when his back was turned?

Pinky clenched his fists again and kept them closed.

No way.

He had reached the top because people were frightened of him. He knew he wouldn't last long if that fear went away. It might have been years ago, but that didn't matter.

JaJa had a lot to lose.

Pinky had more.

26

Milton filtered through the crowd, working his way from one side of the hall to the other. He was adjacent to the ring, next to one of the metal barriers that formed a pathway from the back of the house to the ring. Elijah's opponent was working with his trainer, firing combinations into the pads that were held out in front of him. Milton was impressed: the boxer had good technique, and his punches had power, each one landing with a solid thud.

Connolly finished his workout, stepped through the ropes, and hopped down from the apron. He made his way back along the pathway, passing close enough to Milton that he could have reached out and touched him. His skin was slick with sweat as he touched his gloves to the outstretched fists of the fans outside the barriers.

Tommy Porter took his place in the ring. "Samuel Connolly, ladies and gentlemen," he said. "Our next fighter is Samuel's opponent. With a record of nine fights and nine wins, all by knockout, ladies and gentlemen, let's hear it for one of the hottest prospects in British boxing, the Sheffield Express, Mustafa 'Boom Boom' Muhammad."

There was a loud roar from the crowd, the loudest response that Milton had heard so far. He knew it was just a precursor to what would happen on Saturday night, but even so, he was still surprised at the noise generated for what was, after all, just a workout. Music pounded out of the bass bins as the DJ played a track that Milton didn't recognise, and a spotlight picked out a hooded figure as he made his way out of the doors at the back of the hall and approached the ring between the barriers.

It was Elijah. He wore leopard-skin shorts and pristine white boots. He looked cocky, dance-walking to the ring, glancing over at Milton as he passed and then flicking his eyes away again without acknowledgement. Milton wasn't sure if he had missed him, or whether he had recognised him and ignored him. Elijah was by him in a second, jumping up onto the apron and gripping the top rope with both hands. He leapt up, flipping head over heels as he somersaulted inside, sending the crowd's fervour up a notch. He started to shadow-box, firing out lefts and rights, dancing across the canvas, switching from orthodox to southpaw and back again, completely natural. He jerked to the side and to the front and back like an air dancer, firing out a corkscrewing uppercut that would take off his opponent's head should he land it.

The confidence dripped off him. It was almost tangible. Milton found himself dumbfounded at how much Elijah had changed: he was no longer the shy boy who had been reluctant to let down his guard. Milton had worked hard to win his trust and had been rewarded by a sensitivity that had seemingly been buried now.

Elijah's fists moved with a fluidity that spoke of immense

natural talent; his feet never stopped moving, opening up angles for combinations that would have been impossible to predict, let alone defend. Connolly had been decent enough —he had been solid—but Milton could see now that Elijah would put him to sleep.

Elijah's trainer was a much older man in his late forties, and he came into the ring with the pads. Elijah started to work, firing a barrage of lightning-fast combinations, but Milton's attention was distracted.

It was him.

He checked, trying to confirm his suspicion. A face in the crowd on the other side of the ring, disdainful, staring up at Elijah with a sneer.

Milton recognised him from the pictures.

It was the young man who called himself Pinky.

Close by him was the bigger one, Little Mark, the man from whom Milton had taken the phone.

Between Little Mark and Pinky were the two others whose faces Milton recognised from the pictures Ziggy had found: Chips and Kidz.

The crowd eddied around the four young men, and Milton saw yet more of them. A clutch of them, maybe in their late teens, boisterous and agitated. They wore hooded tops, the hoods up, and bounced with pent-up energy. Milton noticed one thing that they all had in common: the four young men and the teenagers were all wearing purple bandanas, some knotted around their throats, others on their heads. He remembered: it was the uniform of the London Fields Boys.

He knew: it was about to go down.

Shit.

Milton looked back to Pinky and his crew. Kidz and Little Mark were moving away, and the younger boys were going with them. They were coming around the ring, violence in their eyes. It was hard to get an accurate count as they blended through the crowd, but Milton guessed there were ten of them, maybe more. Most of them looked no older than fifteen, but they all looked hardened.

Milton glanced back to the ring. Elijah had finished his workout. He went to the turnbuckle and climbed up to the second rope, his gloved fist held aloft. The spotlight settled on him, cast him in silhouette, and the crowd roared. He responded by raising both fists above his head.

That was when they made their move.

They rushed towards the ring, shouting and screaming, pushing down the people who were in their way. There were security guards on the doors and a couple in the narrow margin between the ring and the crowd, but they were unprepared and they didn't move.

Milton moved, crossing the space, as one of the boys clambered over the security barrier and wriggled beneath the rope and into the ring.

Milton surged ahead.

The boy in the ring got to his feet and took a swing at Elijah. Milton was intent on moving through the crowd and only just caught what happened; there was a blur of green as Elijah cracked a right hook into the side of the boy's head. The boy went down, bouncing off the canvas, but two more were struggling over the barrier, ready to take his place.

"That's enough," the promoter called over the PA, his voice tight with anxiety. "Please—get away from the ring."

Milton was aware of phones being held up, pointing at the ring, but he ignored them. He came face-to-face with a lad of around sixteen. Milton grabbed him around the shoulders and hauled him back. The boy broke away, stumbled, collected his balance, and drew back his fist to throw a punch, but Milton was too quick. He ducked down, sweeping the lad's legs from underneath him. The boy slammed to the wooden floor, gasping as the wind was knocked out of him.

Milton stepped over him and kept moving, spotted another teen with a purple bandana, a security guard holding another one back. A third was trying to get over the barrier, shouting in the face of the guard who was restraining him.

A cacophony of noise.

Bedlam.

And Milton was right in the middle of it.

The crowd contracted, bodies shoved up together, elbows thrown out, punches fired left and right, the little knot of violence spreading through the crowd like waves from a rock dropped into a pool. Milton heard screams and shouts, someone on the floor, a stomp and a kick, more punches, a young man caught in a headlock by a skin-headed guard in a bomber jacket. Milton looked up into the ring and saw Elijah backing away, looking out across the crowd, his eyes wide.

Someone grabbed Milton by the shoulders. It was a hard grip, fingers knotting into the fabric of his jacket, trying to yank him to the side. Milton pivoted, broke the grip, ducked under his assailant's arms, and jammed an elbow into the man's face. It was an older man, not wearing purple. The violence had started to metastasize, infecting the others in the crowd. Milton moved quickly to the side, creating space for himself. There seemed to be more and more of the purple bandanas getting closer to the ring; the promoter yelled out for calm, said the police had been called. He looked ridiculous in his Santa's hat and beard.

Milton remembered the riots from three years earlier,

the backdrop for his reckoning with Bizness. He recalled how quickly things had escalated then. Without warning, he found himself in front of a man he recognised: Little Mark. The big guy hadn't seen him. He was looking over Milton's head towards the developing melee and smirking.

"Hey," Milton said.

Little Mark looked down, his confusion morphing into recognition and then anger.

All too late.

Milton shot out a foot, a sideways kick that terminated in the side of the bigger man's patella. He felt the crunch through the sole of his boot, felt the give as the tendons ripped, and then the bigger man was suddenly on the floor at his feet.

Milton didn't get the chance to admire his handiwork, carried forward by a rush of the crowd.

27

Pinky *loved* it. The disturbance quickly spread as members of other local gangs—the Bethnal Green Massive, the Brick Lane Massive, the E3 Bloods, the Whiston Road Boys and all the others—realised from the purple bandanas that the LFB was in the house and on the attack. Scuffles broke out all the way across the room and quickly overwhelmed the security. The police were on their way, but by the time they arrived, the gangs would have caused all the chaos that he could have wanted. It wouldn't matter then.

He turned to see a young black kid whom he recognised as a member of the Stepney Posse, one of the young bloods who had come over the border into the park a week ago. There had been a scuffle, and Pinky remembered the younger's attitude, bigging up for his mates, making threats and promises when they had seen the police driving across the grass and knowing that nothing could have happened. *Little pussy.* The kid hadn't seen him and, as he took a quarter turn in Pinky's direction, Pinky nailed him with a straight right jab. The boy's nose exploded in a splash of blood and he stumbled back. Pinky felt the buzz in his veins and shook out his knuckles, followed after him and doubled him up with a knee to the groin. He raised his elbow and crashed it down onto the back of the boy's head, collapsing him onto the floor.

Fuckin' A.

He looked up, over the roiling crowd, and gazed over to the ring. The spotlight shining down from the balcony was still on, and, as Pinky watched, JaJa passed through it. One of the LFB crew—a younger called Bars—had made it into the ring with him and the two of them squared up. JaJa disposed of Bars with brutal efficiency, two hooks into his kidneys and then, his guard demolished, a stinging jab that knocked him down. Pinky almost admired him. He had watched his workout with jealousy; he had to admit that the little pussy had something. His hands moved in blurs and his footwork was fast, but that meant nothing, not really, not in real life. JaJa was a boxer, and the flashy entrance and the confident display wouldn't mean a thing back on the street.

Pinky didn't want to confront him today. That wasn't the plan. This wasn't his element; there were others here—witnesses—and security who would get in the way. Things would be different later, when they were back on familiar territory. They'd be alone then, and Pinky would show everyone what happened to those who grassed him up to the police, to those who dissed him, to those who even *looked* at him the wrong way.

Pinky's attention was drawn to Little Mark. The big man was scything his way through the crowd towards the ring, shouldering people out of the way. Pinky saw him stop suddenly, and then watched as a man who was turned away from Pinky kicked down at Little Mark's legs. He dropped to the floor, hidden from Pinky's view by the crowd. The man who had felled him turned around, and Pinky, with open mouth, realised that he had seen him before.

It was the old white guy who had murdered Bizness.

Pinky froze. He was on the other side of the room, separated from him by fifty onlookers, but he still felt a shiver pass up and down his spine. Pinky had never forgotten that night—what he had seen that man do in Bizness's studio, and the way that the man's cold eyes had held him after he'd realised that Pinky had been hiding there.

He heard a commotion from the entrance and turned to see four big policemen bundle their way inside. He looked back at the ring: JaJa was stepping through the ropes and making his way back to the rear of the room from where the fighters had emerged. The white guy was on the move, too, pushing through the ruckus and following.

Pinky backed away.

Time to jet.

28

Some onlookers were trying to move out of the way of the danger, while others were desperate to get a closer look. Milton found himself being swept towards the front, where the younger gang members were still fighting, but now in smaller factions. More security had arrived, and he heard the yells of the police officers, who were rushing in from the other side of the room.

Milton reached the security barrier and saw Elijah being shepherded backstage. He vaulted the barrier and rushed after him. He didn't look like the others and he was wearing a press pass; none of the security tried to stop him as he jogged out of the room and into the backstage area.

Elijah was with his trainer.

"Elijah," Milton shouted, then tried to get closer. His path was blocked by a burly security guard.

He held up the pass and the man stepped aside. He managed to get closer and called out again.

Elijah turned, a frown on his face.

Milton was out of breath. "You all right?"

People moved aside and Elijah stepped closer. His

expression changed again: the frown became wide-eyed recognition and then a scowl of sudden anger.

"Elijah—it's me. John. Do you remember me?"

"Yeah, I remember," Elijah replied, his face inscrutable.

The punch landed with such velocity that Milton was on the floor almost before he had realised what had happened. He fell down onto his side, pain blasting out of his jaw. He tried to raise himself up, bracing his weight on his forearm, and looked around groggily. Elijah was being ushered out of the way, but he turned and trotted backwards so that he could look at what he had done.

The young man's eyes blazed with anger.

29

Milton found an emergency exit at the back of the building, barged the kick plate and stumbled outside. He spat bloody saliva out onto the pavement and groaned at his own naïveté. What did he expect? Elijah had found Rutherford's body and Milton had disappeared. The police had been looking for him; the media had been running appeals for information as to his whereabouts as he had arrived in Manchester, ready to leave the country. What must Elijah have thought? Milton had blown through his life like a hurricane, leaving his mother scarred, his home burned to the ground, and a man who cared about him dead.

Milton wondered: had Sharon even told Elijah that he was back?

He should have guessed that Elijah would not react well. He had told Sharon more about his history when he had first inserted himself into their lives, and she had been prepared to listen to what he had to say yesterday when they had met. Elijah was young and had been suspicious of Milton right from the start. It had taken effort and tact that

Milton hadn't known he possessed to persuade the boy that he could be trusted. It appeared that he would need further convincing, if, indeed, that was even possible at all.

"Fuck it," he said through gritted teeth. Pain throbbed from his jaw. He didn't think it was broken; the wraps on Elijah's hands had cushioned the blow a little, but his fist had still been more than hard enough to do damage. His jaw would be bruised at the very least. He ran his tongue across his teeth, checking that they were still there. All present and correct.

He allowed himself a smile, then winced; smiling was painful. Elijah was everything they said he was, and more. He was fast, his footwork was exemplary, and he could hit.

His phone vibrated in his pocket. He fished it out and saw that it was Sharon.

"Hello, Sharon," he said.

"I was watching the workout on the TV. What happened?"

She was nervous, her words tripping out quickly.

"There was a bit of a scuffle," Milton said, downplaying it. "There were some troublemakers there. It got a little unpleasant, but it's settled down now."

"Is Elijah okay?"

"He's fine. They got him out of the way pretty quickly. Did you speak to him?"

"About?"

"Me coming to see him?"

"I didn't get a chance," she said. "He hasn't been picking up his phone. Why? Did you see him?"

"I said hello," Milton replied.

"And?" She sounded nervous.

"And the hype is true. He's got a punch like a jackhammer."

30

Milton went to a café on the Old Bethnal Green Road and bought a Coke and a coffee. He fished the ice cubes out of the Coke, put them inside a napkin and pressed it against his jaw. He chuckled to himself. He had let his guard down and paid the price. He didn't fancy Connolly's chances if Elijah connected like that on Christmas Eve.

He felt a buzz from his inside pocket. His own phone was on the table: it wasn't that. He reached inside and took out the phone that he had taken from Little Mark. The screen showed an inbound message. Milton tapped in the passcode and opened it.

It was from Pinky.

>> Where you go, pussy? You ran away.

Milton tapped out a reply.

>> Hello Shaquille.

>> We got beef now. Where you at?

>> Why?

>> I want to come see you.

>> That wouldn't be a very good idea.

>> Why? You think I'm scared?

>> You should be.

>> U all talk, old man.

>> Bizness said the same thing. Look what happened to him.

Milton waited for a reply, but none came. Instead, the screen flashed with a message: 'Pinky would like to FaceTime.'

Milton looked around the café. There were other customers there, but no one was paying him any attention. He reached into his pocket for his AirPods, pushed them into his ears, then held his finger over the button to accept the request. He wondered whether it was wise, but decided that he needed to know more.

The screen went dark for a minute and then displayed an image of a young man's face. He had a hook nose and pointed cheekbones, his lips were thin and spiteful, and his eyes shone with a steady hatred. Milton remembered him. The last time he had seen him, just after he had disposed of Bizness, he had been frightened: a fifteen- or sixteen-year-old boy who had just witnessed a man's murder.

He didn't look frightened now. He looked angry.

"I was a boy back then," he said. "I didn't know shit. I ain't a boy now."

"No," Milton said quietly. "You're not a boy. But you're still out of your depth."

He laughed. "Look at yourself! You're an old white guy in these ends and you say I'm out of my depth? Are you mental? You gonna get dooked! Where is that? Where are you?"

Pinky moved the phone down a little, and Milton caught a glimpse of a darkened room, the harsh light from a naked bulb smearing across the screen until the exposure adjusted. Milton saw a door and a window, partially covered by curtains with a line of dim light down the middle from where they were parted. There was nothing that would give away his location.

"I know about you," Milton said.

"Don't chat shit. You don't. You don't know *nothing* about me."

"I know your name is Shaquille. I know where you live. I know where you do your business—the houses and flats you use. I know your friends—their names, where they are. How's Little Mark? How's his leg?"

Pinky sneered, but Milton saw a flicker of uncertainty. "You're full of it, grandad. You must think I'm stupid. Mark told me you took his phone. You think I'm going to accept your request, let you know where I'm at?"

"Stay away from Elijah, Shaquille. I'm asking nicely. I won't ask nicely again."

Pinky pointed the phone away from his face and moved it back so that he could bring his spare hand into shot. He was holding a Mac-10.

"You know what this is?"

"I do," Milton said.

Pinky held up the submachine gun. "Tell me what to do again and see what happens."

"There's nothing you can say or do that I haven't seen before. I—"

"You all talk, old man!"

Pinky's face crumpled with anger, and he ended the call before Milton could speak again.

Milton stared at the phone. He wondered how the young man—not much more than a boy—could have become so full of hate and spite. Milton did not want to hurt him, but he was starting to think that a confrontation was inevitable.

He tried to put himself in Pinky's shoes, tried to imagine what it must feel like to see a boy like Elijah, someone he had grown up with, doing so well for himself. To think about his potential, the money he might make, the fame, the women. It was easy to see how he would react: with jealousy, rage and frustration. A toxic stew that threatened to boil over, poisoning everything that it touched. Milton felt pity for him, but that would count for nothing if he came at Elijah. Milton would put him down without thinking twice.

The phone buzzed again with an incoming text.

>> FU, lighty. I see you next time and...

The text concluded with an emoji of a gun.

Milton switched the phone off and put it back in his pocket.

Events were gaining momentum. He doubted that he would be able to stop them now; he would react to them instead.

31

Milton had told Sharon to stop apologising. That hadn't really worked and she had insisted that they meet. Milton said that wasn't necessary, but she had been adamant. She gave him the address of her hotel, and he said that he would come to see her at eight o'clock.

Milton arrived fifteen minutes early and found an empty table in the bar. It was ten minutes past eight by the time she walked through the door; a blast of winter air rippled through the room and people glanced over at her and frowned at the draught that she had let in.

Milton raised a hand and she came over.

"Oh, my goodness," she said as soon as she saw his face.

Milton had looked in the mirror earlier: his jaw was one nasty, livid bruise.

He stood for her and smiled. "It's not as bad as it looks."

"I'm so sorry," she said. "Are you okay?"

He flexed his jaw. "Really—I'm fine."

She reached across the table and touched the side of his

face. "He's such a hothead," she said. "I tried to talk to him, but he said he didn't have time."

"He didn't know I was coming?"

"I said you'd been in touch—there wasn't time for anything else. He didn't know you'd be there."

"It's okay," Milton said, understanding a little better why Elijah had reacted the way that he had. "He was surprised. And, anyway, I deserved it."

"You didn't," she protested. "He's young. He's had a difficult few years, and he still doesn't know who to trust. What happened before—you know what he was like then. Mixed up. And we don't talk about what happened that often. He gets angry."

"He still thinks I had something to do with what happened to Rutherford."

Sharon smiled thinly towards him. "I know you didn't. You helped me. You helped Elijah. Your heart is good."

Milton didn't reply to that. It wasn't true.

"I need to see him before Saturday," he said instead, holding up a hand to stop Sharon from interrupting. "I know you don't want him distracted."

"He won't agree."

"He needs to know I'm on his side. I won't be able to help him if he doesn't trust me."

"You think he needs help?"

"I don't know," Milton admitted, not sure of how much he should tell her. He decided that there should be no secrets between them. "I went to your old flat when I arrived. One of the boys from before was there—Little Mark."

"Edwin," she said. "I knew his mother."

"They know about Elijah. You were right. They're jealous about it."

"Pinky?"

"Yes," Milton said. "He was at the workout. Him, Little Mark, the others."

She shuddered. "Oh no."

"They're just young lads, Sharon. I can help Elijah, but I do need to speak to him."

"Okay," she replied finally after a few seconds of silence. "I'll see what I can do."

PART X

THE THIRD DAY

32

Milton's jaw still ached the day after the workout. It wasn't broken, but it still throbbed. The kid had power. Milton corrected himself: Elijah wasn't a kid anymore. He was nineteen years old, a man, with all the responsibility and pressure that came with it.

He took an Uber from the hotel to Plaistow. The city became less affluent the farther east they travelled; the houses were cheaper, the shops less ostentatious, yet there was more life here. There were open-air markets with stalls selling clothes, others offering batteries and household goods, refrigerated vans where traders offered cuts of beef straight out of the back. They passed into West Ham, and Milton told the driver to stop opposite the florist that he had noticed on the other side of the road. He hopped out, picked a path through the slow-moving queue of traffic on the other side of the road, and went inside the shop. The atmosphere was heady with fresh blooms; Milton pointed to a bucket of roses and asked for a bouquet. He paid the proprietor and made his way back to the waiting car.

"All good?" the driver asked him.

"All good."

They skirted the Memorial Playing Ground until they reached the East London Cemetery. He had been meaning to come here all week. Milton thanked the driver, taking out his phone to rate him and leave a tip. He passed between the double piers of an open gate and made his way along the central drive that led to the chapel. He looked left and right and saw thousands of graves.

Milton had looked on Wikipedia during the drive across town: the cemetery had been established in the 1870s to accommodate the increasing demand for space from the city and the surrounding boroughs. It was the final resting place for Karl Hans Lody, the last person to have been shot as a spy in the Tower of London. That, he thought, and the death all around, seemed apt.

He had asked Ziggy to find the grave that he wanted. Now he found the aisle that Ziggy had indicated in the northwest corner of the cemetery and walked slowly along it, his eyes cast down at the headstones. It took him ten minutes to find it.

In Loving Memory of Son & Brother Dennis Rutherford.

The simple marble headstone had been maintained, and Milton saw that a bouquet, still wrapped in plastic, had been left on the grave in the last few days. He knelt down and rested his hand on the cold stone, laying his own bouquet next to the one that was already there.

"I'm sorry," he said quietly.

He stayed there for a moment, his eyes closed. He listened to the birdsong and, in the distance, the sound of someone tilling the ground. He stood, his knees creaking, and made his way back to the gates.

33

Milton looked at his watch. It was ten o'clock. He looked back up and saw that a man was waiting by the gates.

"Punctual as ever," Milton said as he drew near enough to be heard.

"That's the army for you. Old habits die hard."

Alex Hicks grinned and put out his hand. Milton took it and allowed himself to be drawn into a hug. Hicks clapped him on the back.

"Jesus," Hicks said. "What happened to your face?"

Milton instinctively reached up for his jaw. "Yes," he said. "That. I'll tell you about it in a minute. Want a coffee?"

THERE WAS a café a short distance from the cemetery, and Milton led the way there. It was empty, and Hicks took one of the Formica tables as Milton ordered. He looked back at his old friend. There was nothing particularly distinctive about Hicks's appearance: short hair kept close to the scalp, medium build, athletic rather than muscular, average height. He looked just like a typical special forces operator, appropriate given that he and Milton had both been in the Regiment together. Hicks had been tapped as a possible recruit for the Group, and Milton had been responsible for assessing him. He was an outstanding soldier, but Milton had detected an underlying goodness running through him and had recommended that he be passed over. Milton had been in the depths of his own self-loathing then and had dismissed Hicks because he had seen something admirable in him. Milton had been unable to sully that. He couldn't drag Hicks down into the blood and the dirt with the other killers who made up the Group.

He put the coffees onto the table and sat down. "Thanks for coming."

"Not a problem."

Milton had helped Hicks extricate himself from an entanglement several years earlier, and Hicks had made it clear that he considered himself to be in his debt. Milton had told Hicks that he owed him nothing, but Hicks, apparently, did not agree.

"It's Christmas," Milton said. "You have kids."

"They're going to the cinema. They won't miss me."

"Still, I appreciate it. What did you tell Rachel?"

"That you need a hand with something. You know what she thinks about you, John. She would have killed me if I *didn't* come."

Hicks's wife had been fighting cancer for several years. A lack of money for her treatment was what had forced Hicks into the compromising situation from which Milton had extricated him, and then Milton had helped find the money to pay for the treatment.

"How is she?"

"Still in remission," Hicks said. "She's tested twice a year. We're all over it."

"Good."

They sipped their drinks.

"So," Hicks said with a smile. "What's so important that you needed to spoil my Christmas?"

"Do you follow boxing?"

"Not really."

"There's a young fighter—Mustafa Muhammad."

Hicks frowned. "I've heard of him. Supposed to be good?"

"He's *very* good," Milton corrected. "He's fighting on Christmas Eve. Biggest fight of his career."

"And what does he have to do with you?"

"I know him," Milton said. "Met him a few years ago. His real name is Elijah Warriner. He was in trouble—got in with the wrong crowd, went off the rails. I tried to put him straight."

Hicks sipped the coffee. "And?"

"And I nearly did. I got him into boxing, anyway. But this was when I was trying to leave the Group. Control sent one of the others after me. I was shot, and the man I introduced Elijah to was killed. I had to run. Elijah thought—probably still thinks—that I did it. I've never really forgotten about him, or his mother. They're good people. They had a lot of bad luck that they didn't deserve."

"And now?" Hicks said.

"The kids he used to run around with are jealous. I think they're going to cause trouble. There was a scuffle at a workout yesterday, and I think that was just the start. There's one of them in particular—I had a conversation with him yesterday, and he made it very clear that he considers that they have unfinished business. I think something's going to happen this week—either before the fight or after it."

"So can you look after him?"

"I tried that." Milton pointed to the side of his face again.

"That was him?"

Milton nodded. "He's going to be hard for me to reach. And it's just me. I don't think I'd be able to do it alone."

"Fine. I'm in. What do you need me to do?"

"Thank you." Milton wasn't surprised that Hicks had volunteered, but that didn't mean that he wasn't grateful. "I need you to follow him. He'll recognise me. He doesn't trust me enough to let me get close."

"But he doesn't know me."

"Exactly."

"For how long?"

"The next couple of days. The fight's on Christmas Eve. He'll be out of the city after that."

Hicks nodded. "How observant is he?"

"He's no fool."

"So it's just me on him?"

"No," Milton said. "We have backup."

"We do?"

Milton gestured over to the door. A hunched figure pushed it open and stepped into the café. He had a hood over his head and a rucksack hooked over his shoulder.

Hicks groaned. "Seriously?"

"Be nice," Milton said.

"You're that desperate?"

The figure reached up and pulled down the hood.

"Look at this," Ziggy said. "The band's back together."

34

Sol had an apartment halfway up the old Centrepoint building. Pinky had texted him and said that he wanted to meet; Sol had told him to come over.

Everyone recognised the old building, one of the first skyscrapers to go up in west London, and he had heard that Sol had bought an apartment just after the place had been converted from offices to residential. Pinky had googled for details in the back of the Uber and had gawped at how much the apartments were going for: they started at £1.8m for a small one-bedroom apartment and went all the way up to £55m for the penthouses on the top floor.

Pinky gazed out of the car window as the building loomed overhead and shook his head in wonder: everyone knew Sol was smart, but there was smart and then there was million-pound-apartment smart. Bizness had never managed anything like this. Maybe his brother had got the brains in the family.

Pinky went into the lobby. It was all glitz and glamour, steel and smoked glass with a weird-looking crystal chandelier suspended over a broad flight of stairs that went up to the first floor. He felt out of place here, like he was somewhere he wasn't supposed to be. He guessed that was the point of it all: the people who lived here had the money to feel special, and they were happy to make it known that they were better than everyone else. Pinky reached down, hiked up his low-slung jeans, and slouched over to the desk.

"I'm here to see Solomon Brown," he said.

The man looked down his nose at him, and, for a moment, Pinky thought that he was going to ask him to leave.

"Name?"

"Shaquille."

"Mr. Brown said you should go straight up," the man said. He told Pinky to take the lift to the tenth floor and then make his way to apartment 1016.

Pinky went across the lobby and pressed the button for the lift. He was sweating and his finger left a smear of grease on the polished metal. Good. He reached out with his hand, pressed all four fingers and thumb on the gleaming elevator door, and drew them down, five trails of grease spoiling the perfect shine.

The elevator opened and he stepped inside. He pressed the button for the tenth floor and leaned against the wall as the car ascended. The walls and ceiling were mirrored; Pinky looked at his reflection, put his shoulders back and his chin out. His gold chain glittered in the artificial light. He looked good, he thought. He could imagine himself in a place like this. It was beyond him now, of course, but who would have thought he would rise so quickly through the LFB in such a short space of time? He wasn't a fool: he had been no one before, a no-account younger just like all the others. He had worked hard to ingratiate himself with the elders, with Bizness and his bloods; he had taken their shit, gone to Maccy D's to pick up their food, ran their errands, all so he could bring himself closer to them, inch by inch by inch. He hated having to suck up to them, to take their jibes and jokes, but he knew it was a means to an end, and that the end would be worth it. That was what had annoyed him so much about JaJa—how the little bitch had caught Bizness's eye and got closer to him in days than Pinky had managed in months. Fuck *that*, he thought now.

Fuck all this, he decided. It was taking too long. He wanted this *now*, not in five years.

He hadn't been ambitious enough. That was going to change.

THE ELEVATOR REACHED the tenth floor, and Pinky found his way along the corridor to the door for 1016. He took a breath to settle his nerves and rapped his knuckles against the door.

It opened. A woman was standing inside. She was fit, dressed in clothes that Pinky could tell were expensive, her skin smooth, her brows plucked into two neat diagonals.

"Come in," she said.

"I'm here for Sol."

"I know. He's just having a shower. Go through into the living room. There's beer in the fridge if you want one."

Pinky went inside. There was an entrance hall, what looked like a bedroom and then a larger living area and kitchen. The floor of the hall was tiled in a pattern that Pinky guessed was designed to look like the outside of the building; he went through into the living room and gaped at the huge expanse of glass and the view outside, London laid out far below, its lights glittering magically.

He sat down on a chair that looked more suited for display than comfort, took out his phone, and watched the footage again, unable to keep the smile from his face. Everything had gone just how he wanted it to. The youngers had done their job well, he thought. They'd caused mayhem, and, by the time the police had come to close it all down, fights had started between members of all the local gangs. They had instigated it, then let natural enmities take their course. Lots of brothers in the same place, amped up after watching the boys in the ring, a powder keg ready to explode. All he'd had to do was light the match.

His thoughts ran to the old man and his mood soured. They'd put Little Mark in a cab and told the driver to take him to the hospital. Brother couldn't put any weight on his right leg. Pinky watched plenty of football, and he knew there was all sorts of shit that could go wrong inside someone's knee. Zlatan had torn up his ACL, and he had been on the shelf for months. He'd never been the same, not even on FIFA. Little Mark said that the old guy had known exactly what he was doing, dropping down out of the way and then hitting him with 'kung fu shit.'

Pinky thought of the conversation he'd had with the man on the phone. He remembered him from before. The man had broken into Bizness's place on the night of the riot, shot him down, and then put a cushion over his face and suffocated him. Pinky had been hiding, pressed down against the floor behind a sofa as the bullets from Bizness's machine gun tore up the place. The man had taken the cushion away from Bizness's face and had looked up and seen him.

Pinky remembered: his expression had been dead, as if what he had just done meant nothing to him at all. He was cold—a killer—and Pinky had thought about him a lot ever since that night.

Pinky wasn't scared. He was a killer, too. They had that shit in common, but now the man was back, putting his nose into other people's business again, and there would be consequences.

Pinky had decided before they had spoken on the phone: the man was going to have to get done.

He looked at his watch. He had been waiting for ten minutes. He felt a twist of impatience in his gut. Sol was keeping him waiting to make a point. That shit was *childish*. He told himself not to get worked up about it.

35

The weigh-in had been scheduled for York Hall with the public in attendance, but after what had happened at the workout, that had all been changed. It was now to be held at the hotel that had staged the press conference, and the audience had been restricted to the press.

Milton had spoken to Sharon on the telephone earlier, and she had said that Elijah would meet him at the back of the hotel once the weigh-in was concluded. She said that she had managed to convince her son to speak to him for a few minutes. He would hear him out, but there were no promises. Milton didn't know if it would be enough time, but he wanted to try.

Milton made his way to the passage behind the hotel in plenty of time. He waited for over an hour before the back door opened and people began to leave. He stepped away from the wall he was leaning against and stood ready for Elijah to emerge.

Finally, Milton saw him. He was dressed in a black tracksuit with a hood over his head. He was drinking from a water bottle and had headphones draped around his neck. He wore black sunglasses even though the clouds were iron grey overhead and there was the promise of snow in the air.

Milton stepped away from the wall.

Elijah came up to him.

"You going to hit me again?" Milton said.

"I should do more than that," Elijah replied. His jaw was set and a tic pulsed in his cheek. "You deserved it."

"I didn't do what you think I did," Milton said, looking into the black lenses that hid Elijah's eyes.

"Not what the papers said."

"I know," Milton said.

"The police, too. They know you're here?"

"No," Milton said. "They don't."

"So?"

"I told your mum what happened."

"Yeah," he said. "She told me." He dismissed that, and anything that Sharon might have said to him, with a wave of his hand. "You remember when we had dinner in Nando's?"

"Yes," Milton said.

"You remember what I asked you?"

"You asked me what I did for a job."

"That's right. And you remember what you said?"

"Not exactly."

"I do," he said. "I remember it like yesterday. You said you were a problem solver. Except that's not what you were, was it? You caused more problems than you solved. My mum got burned. Rutherford got it worse—he got shot. Even if you didn't do it, he's still dead and it's still your fault."

Milton remembered that conversation. It had been three years ago, and Elijah had changed so much in that time. He had been a boy then, reticent, suspicious, and difficult to reach. Milton had worked so hard to earn his trust, and that was the moment when he had felt that he had finally been successful. But he knew there was no point in pretending otherwise: he hadn't done what he had promised, and he had probably caused problems that could otherwise have been avoided. Elijah had a point.

"It wasn't supposed to happen like that. I wanted to help you. I wanted to help your mother."

"So she said."

"She tell you everything?"

"What do you mean?"

"She tell you where she and I were the first time we met?"

Elijah paused. "No," he said. "What difference does that make?"

"She jumped onto the tracks in front of a train," Milton said. "I pulled her out of the way before it could hit her. I took her to the hospital, and then, when they let her out, I brought her home."

Elijah's jaw slackened as the anger and tension dripped away to be replaced by something else. Milton couldn't see his eyes behind the shades, and he couldn't gauge his reaction. "What?" he said quietly, the hardness gone.

"I didn't tell you before," Milton said. "I didn't see what good it would do. But maybe you need to know. Do you know why she did it?"

Elijah looked down at his feet.

"You and your brother," Milton said. "She was at the end of her rope. I know what it's like to feel desperate—I felt the same way then. You still want to know what I used to do? The truth this time?"

Elijah nodded.

"I used to work for the government. There would occasionally be situations when a problem would arise that couldn't be solved in the usual way. I'll give you an example: a British agent looking into the mafia is murdered in Italy. The authorities over there can't or won't do anything about it. I was the person who was sent to find out what happened and to make sure it never happened again."

"'Make sure it never happened again'? What does that mean?"

"I'm sure you can join the dots, Elijah."

"You killed people?"

Milton still didn't want to say it. "I did things that I thought were right at the time, but now I'm not so sure. I left that job just before I met you. I was in a mess. I was sick with guilt. I saw your mum and I wanted to help her."

"Thought it would make you feel better?"

"Maybe," he admitted. "But I thought it was the right thing to do. I'm trying to do the right thing with my life, with however long I have left. Did I fuck it up with you? Probably. But I did what I did for the right reasons."

Milton still couldn't see whether he was getting through to him.

"You still haven't told me what happened to Rutherford."

"Like I said—I quit my job. Unfortunately, the agency I used to work for wasn't happy about that. They decided that this time I was the problem, and they sent a man to sort it out. He found me in the gym the night you had that bout. I stayed late to work on the electrics. Rutherford came back. He wasn't supposed to be there."

"He forgot to set the alarm," Elijah mumbled. "Said you'd set it off."

"The man shot him, but Rutherford gave me the distraction I needed to save myself."

"And then you just ran?"

"I know what that looks like."

"Like you're guilty," Elijah said. "Or a *coward*."

"I had no choice. He shot me, too, and I knew that they would just send others to finish the job. So I ran."

Elijah didn't speak.

"Listen to me, Elijah," he said. "I took you to Rutherford for a reason. Look at where that's taken you. I respected him. I was trying to help him. I didn't kill him."

Elijah took a step towards Milton. He took off his sunglasses and hooked them in the neckline of his jacket. "Look at you," he said. "You claiming credit for what Rutherford did? You introduced me to him. Fair enough. But that's it. He recognised what was inside me. He was in my life for a few weeks, but he changed me forever. Set me on the right path. And now, because of what you did or didn't do, he ain't here to see where that got me. You haven't even said why you're here."

"Because you're in trouble."

"The kids from the estate? Yeah, I saw them at the workout. I ain't worried about them. What they gonna do?"

Milton felt the anger steaming from the young man. That's what he was. A young man who had had no choice but to grow up too quickly, and now he was filled with nothing but hurt and pain.

"I think they're dangerous," Milton said. "At least one of them has a gun. I'm worried about you. And I'd like to help."

"Like last time?" He shook his head emphatically. "I don't want it." He stepped up until he was just a few inches from Milton. "You owe me, you owe us all, but we don't want it. You stay away from us. Don't talk to my mum; don't try to help me."

"Elijah—"

"Nah, man. It's all about you, trying to make yourself feel

good, but you don't deserve it. All you did last time was mess up our lives. You might not have pulled the trigger, but a good man is dead because of you. What's next? You gonna fuck up the good thing I've got going? Thanks, but no thanks. Those boys got something coming for me, I'll deal with it. I don't need you."

A young woman came out of the door. She was pretty: black skin, long black hair, large black glasses over her eyes. She stood at the end of the alley and then started towards the two of them.

"Elijah—" Milton said.

"I ain't asking, I'm telling. Stay the *fuck* away. You don't, you keep putting your nose in my business, next time I'll make sure you don't get back up again."

The woman reached them. She smiled at Milton, but before she could speak, Elijah took her by the hand and led her away. He whistled and a black cab pulled up at the side of the road. Elijah opened the door for the woman and then followed her inside.

Milton walked up to the kerb as the cab drove away. He took out his phone and called the number that he had saved.

"You got the car?"

"I got it," Hicks said. "Leave it to me."

36

Pinky looked at his watch. He had been inside the flat for twenty minutes and he was still waiting for Sol. He knew what was happening: Sol was making him wait to let him know who was in charge, that Pinky might have been an elder but he was still nothing, no one, a nobody. He clenched his teeth and looked around the room, wondering what Sol would do if he put his fist through that sixty-inch TV on the wall, how long it would take him to get his arse in here if he did something like that.

The door opened and Sol came inside.

"Sorry, man," he said, grinning, obviously not sorry at all. "Busy with my girl—know what I'm saying?"

He grinned again, revealing a flash of gold inside his mouth, and Pinky was reminded of Bizness. He had treated Pinky the same—dismissed him, talked down to him—and look what had happened to him. Pinky was still here, though. He was a survivor.

"You see what happened yesterday?" Pinky said.

"Nah," Sol said, dropping down onto the sofa. "What happened yesterday?"

Pinky took out his phone, opened YouTube, and handed it to the older man. "At the workout they had," he said, explaining. "Me and some of the others took a bunch of youngers down, smashed the place up."

Sol frowned as he looked at the screen in his hand.

Pinky paused, then said, "You see?"

"What the *fuck?*"

"What do you mean?" Pinky said, confused.

Sol surged out of the sofa and flung Pinky's phone against the wall.

"What—"

Pinky didn't get the chance to finish the sentence. Sol grabbed his shirt in both fists and hauled him up, pushing him all the way across the room until he crashed against the window. Sol leaned in, pressing hard, then raised his arm like a bar and pressed it against Pinky's throat.

"Who told you to do that?"

Pinky struggled to draw breath. "No one..." he started.

"Did *I* tell you to do something so fucking stupid?"

"I thought—"

"You *thought?* You don't *do* the thinking, you little prick." He pushed harder. "What? You think you're a badman now? You think you're gangster? You ain't gangster. You ain't nothing. You a little bitch who got ideas above his station."

Sol pressed harder and, for a moment, Pinky wondered whether it was possible that the glass would shatter and he would be shoved outside to his death. But then Sol leaned away from the glass, pivoted on one leg, and sent Pinky flying back across the room.

Pinky got to his feet. "I don't get it. What did we do wrong?"

"You think that's enough?" Sol said. "Just a bit of a scuffle and that's it? You think that's good enough for what I want?"

"I never said that—"

"What did you think it'd do for us? Tell me."

Pinky blinked at him. "They know who Elijah is now. Where he's from. All those things he's been chatting—everyone will see they're just lies. They'll find out he's from these ends, that he ain't nothing but a nasty little hood rat. How's it gonna look to all those white boys in suits on the telly? The money men? They know what he is now."

Sol listened quietly, but Pinky could see that he was moments away from another explosion of rage.

"Do I have to spell it out for you? We want him to win. We want him to make money. We're going to make money *off* him, you little idiot. If he's as good as they say he is, he's the golden goose. We get into him like I know we can get into him, we could make *millions*."

Pinky reached for the one thing that he knew would calm Sol down.

"There's something else," he said.

"What?"

"The guy who killed Bizness."

Sol took a beat. "What about him?"

"You know I saw him. Before. When it happened."

"So you say."

"He was there."

Sol was on him again, one hand pressing him down to the sofa. "What you say?"

Pinky could feel his warm spittle on his face. "Get the fuck off me, Sol."

Sol leaned back, letting him go.

"He was at the workout. I saw him. I took his picture. It's him."

"You're sure?"

Pinky nodded. "I ain't never going to forget that man's face."

"He's back and you didn't tell me?"

"I'm telling you now."

"Where is he?"

"I don't know. But he has a thing for JaJa. Looks out for him. He saw what happened. He warned me off."

"You spoke to him?"

"He took Little Mark's phone. Mark didn't tell me until yesterday. I called him up. He'll be there for the fight. You want him, that's where he'll be."

Sol rubbed his head. "We can't do nothing at the fight. Too many people." He closed his eyes and breathed out. "He's tight with Elijah?"

"Used to be," Pinky said. "He sounded like he was looking out for him."

"So Elijah knows how to find him."

Sol dropped down onto the sofa, leaned forward, and began rolling a joint on the coffee table as if nothing had happened. There was silence apart from the flick of a lighter, a long slow drawing of breath, then the exhalation of smoke into the air. Pinky went to collect his phone; it wasn't broken. He scrolled back through the YouTube footage until he found the frame he wanted: the older white man making his way through the crowd towards the back. Whoever had shot and uploaded the video had been near him, close enough that there could be no doubt it was him.

Pinky handed the phone to Sol.

"You sure?"

"I'm sure."

Sol handed the phone back and sat back on the sofa, a smile playing across his lips. He handed Pinky the joint and encouraged him to finish it off.

"Maybe this works after all. Two birds, one stone."

The violence of just moments earlier was gone; Sol was like a different man now. Pinky dragged on the joint, holding it in his lungs, letting the fumes take him out of himself. It was black gold, high-potency weed, but it didn't relax him; it helped him focus.

PART XI

THE SECOND DAY

37

It was the day before Christmas, but that hadn't stopped the crowds coming out. Eight thousand men and women made their way through the Olympic Park, all of them looking forward to the five bouts that made up the evening's card. Milton watched them file into the Copper Box Arena. It wasn't particularly festive—twelve young men seeking to knock seven bells out of their opponents—but it did promise to be exciting. He listened to the comments of the spectators in the queue around him; the two main topics of conversation were the disturbance at the workout and whether Mustafa Muhammad really was as good as advertised.

Boxing had changed in the years since Milton had last witnessed a live fight night. It had been a working-class sport when he'd been a younger man. Now, though, it was attended by men in suits and women in dresses, as if it were a night out on the town rather than a sporting event. Milton found it incongruous and not entirely to his liking.

He was wearing his AirPods and opened a conference call to Hicks and Ziggy.

"Where are you both?" he said quietly, his head angled away from the others in the crowd.

"Inside," Hicks said. *"I can't see anything unusual."*

"I'm in the car," Ziggy reported. *"I'm online, good connection. I should be able to back you up from here."*

"Stay sharp," Milton said.

Music was booming from inside the arena. Milton reached the head of the queue and held up his press pass. The guard glanced at it, giving it the most cursory scrutiny, and waved him inside. The crowd was required to pass through scanners, a measure that would at least make it more difficult to bring a weapon inside. There would be other ways into the building that a clever antagonist could exploit, but there was little that could be done about that. Milton and Hicks would just have to stay alert.

The spectators were making their way into the arena through a line of doors on the right-hand side of the corridor that led away from the central area. Milton looked left and found another corridor that was guarded by a yellow-shirted security guard. Milton went up to the man, showed him his pass, and stepped around him. The corridor was full of people moving back and forward, some with cameras filming interviews with various attendees. Milton could feel the tension in the air. The undercard was under way, and the noise was growing by the second.

"Anything?" he said.

"Nothing," Hicks said. He had bought a front-row seat from a tout, and Milton could hear the thud of punches and the cheers of the crowd.

Milton moved around the building, familiarising himself with the entrances and exits, looking for weaknesses. Nothing was obvious and there was a lot of security, no doubt as a result of the fracas earlier in the week. He reached the dressing rooms; pieces of A4 paper with the names of the fighters printed on them had been stuck to the doors.

Milton looked at his watch. Elijah would be fighting in a couple of hours. He slipped past the dressing room with Samuel Connolly's name on the door, then continued onwards until he found Elijah's. He found a space behind a row of metal equipment cases where he could observe without easily being seen. He waited as the doors for both fighters opened and closed. The usual complement of people passed into and out of the dressing rooms: the trainers, the cut-men, the hangers-on. More time passed and the referee came to talk to Connolly and then Elijah.

"Hicks," Milton said, "how's it going?"

"Won't be long," Hicks reported. *"This one is about to end. It's a mismatch. One of them..."* He stopped, and Milton heard a roar from the crowd. *"There you go,"* Hicks continued. *"Knockout. It's over."*

Milton looked up and noticed a woman making her way to Elijah's door. He recognised her: she was the woman he had seen after the weigh-in, the woman who had got into the car with Elijah. Hicks had said that she had gone into the hotel with Elijah, but that he hadn't been able to get close enough to take a decent photo. Milton raised his phone and, as surreptitiously as he could, snapped off a burst.

"Ziggy," he said.

"Go ahead."

"I'm sending you a photo of a woman I want you to check out. I'm sending it now."

He selected the best picture and messaged it to Ziggy's number.

"Got it," he said. *"She's pretty. What do you need?"*

"Anything you can find."

"Will do."

The door to Connolly's dressing room opened, and Milton heard the sound of music thundering from inside. The fighter came out dressed in a cream robe, the hood pulled up to cover his face. He shadow-boxed, his blood-red gloves flashing as he threw out lefts and rights. His entourage came next and, once they were ready, a woman with an earpiece and a microphone ushered them towards the large door that would lead to the walkway between the seating to the ring.

It was time to fight.

38

Elijah was ready.

This was it. The moment everything changed. He stood behind the curtain, feeling the weight of the gloves on his hands, the comforting familiarity of routine. He was at the edge of *his* moment, feeling the energy from the crowd inside the arena as he waited for his music to kick in.

His entourage were gathered around him, but they were forgotten now. He was focused.

The first beat of Stormzy's 'Big for Your Boots' rumbled out of the venue's PA. Elijah bumped his gloves together and started to box, firing out a flurry of lefts and rights, sharp jabs and hooks, left and right, taking his weight on the balls of his feet and bouncing in time. He clenched his jaw.

McCauley looked at him, staring right into his eyes. "Ready?"

There was no need to speak. Elijah nodded. McCauley pulled the curtain aside, and Elijah looked into the arena. It was full, with spotlights swinging across a sea of expectant faces. A walkway extended from the open door to the ring. A scaffold of lights had been suspended over it, bathing it in harsh white. Connolly was there, dancing across the canvas.

The crowd was noisy and, as they saw Elijah, the volume rose. He stepped up and raised his hands. He shadow-boxed as smoke billowed from a dry ice machine, felt hands on his shoulders, and started walking to the ring.

He barely heard the cheers and the boos. There was only one thing in his mind now. Had to be. This was his moment. All the work he had put in had been leading to this. He was live on television, before thousands of people, everyone waiting to see if he could back up his talent.

There was just one person standing in his way.

He reached the ring, clambered up onto the apron, and put his hands on the top rope. He took a breath, feeling the strength in his legs, and sprang up and forward, somersaulting inside and landing smoothly on the canvas. The crowd roared its approval.

"This is it," McCauley said, slipping the white robe off his shoulders and smearing Vaseline across his face. "We've trained hard for this. You have it inside you—just let it out. He can't handle your power or your speed. You know that. Box smart."

McCauley continued talking, but Elijah had heard it all before. It was a reminder. McCauley knew that. It was a familiar voice to calm him down enough so that he could do what he needed to do.

Elijah bounced up and down, waiting and waiting for the bell to ring. The announcer took over.

"In the blue corner, the challenger, weighing in at twelve stones seven pounds even. He boasts a record of nine fights, nine wins by KO. He is the fighting pride of Sheffield—Mustafa 'Boom Boom' Muhammad."

The crowd went crazy, screaming and cheering. Elijah could hear nothing but noise now as he lifted his arms in the air and acknowledged the crowd.

"And in the red corner, weighing in at twelve stones six pounds and three ounces, with a perfect record of eighteen fights, no defeats and fourteen wins by KO. He is the British and Commonwealth champion, the Tottenham Terminator, Samuel 'Lights Out' Connolly."

Elijah stared across the ring as Connolly raised his arms in the air. He looked bigger than he had at the weigh-in, but Elijah knew that he was the larger of the pair. He carried more power, too, even if he was six years younger.

Elijah knew it. He was a freak. A nineteen-year-old kid in a man's body.

Fast.

Powerful.

He was the man.

And he was going to win.

They were ushered to the centre of the ring by their trainers, and the referee delivered his final instructions. Elijah nodded that he understood what he had been told, even if all that he had heard was a faint buzzing, an incoherence lost amid the growing clamour of the spectators. McCauley slapped him on the cheek, pushed in his mouth-guard, squeezed his shoulders, and left him alone.

It was him, Connolly and the referee.

That was it.

It was easy to feel alone, and Elijah welcomed it.

Everything else was forgotten. Every detail of his life leading to that moment. All the hurt and pain he had suffered. All the bad, all the good. His family, his friends. They all faded away until there was only a single point of focus.

Samuel Connolly.

The bell rang.

39

Milton found his way to the press box. It was part of the balcony, a closed box fronted by a wide picture window. There were two rows of seats, one raised above the other, and each seat came with a small retractable desk. The print journalists were there, their laptops out, already tapping out their thoughts as they waited for the bell. Milton looked to the right and saw a second box that had been given over to the television coverage, with a small studio and, next to it, a space for the commentator and the colour man.

All the seats were taken. Milton stayed at the back of the room and looked down through the window to the ring below.

The bell rang.

"Here we go," someone muttered. "Let's see what he's got."

Milton watched. Elijah moved to the centre of the ring and flicked out a jab as Connolly met him there. He caught a jab from Connolly on his right glove, countered with another of his own. He moved around, firing out the jab and finding his range. Connolly was rangier than Milton had expected. He had long arms and his fists moved quickly, but Elijah had started well. He was concentrating on the movement in front of him, wary of incoming artillery even as he landed his own punches.

Milton found that he had clenched his own fists, and that he was twitchy with nerves. Elijah stepped back, too slow, and caught a jab flush in the face. He stumbled, just a little, then came back with a three-shot combination that sent Connolly back to the ropes.

Come on, Milton thought. *Go get him.*

The bell rang before Elijah could follow up.

ELIJAH MADE his way back to the corner, sitting down on the stool and opening his mouth so that his mouthguard could be removed. His heart was beating faster than it normally did after one round.

"Boxing well, Mustafa," McCauley said, talking fast. "Keep finding your range and don't forget the jab to the body. He's moving well, but you can move better, you hear me?"

Elijah nodded, glancing at ringside and seeing the blurred faces gawping back at him. He blinked and saw them all in focus again. Men in suits. Women in dresses. *Money.*

"One down," McCauley continued, tipping a water bottle into his mouth and wiping his face down. "You've got him. He's good, but you're better. When you land, he won't be able to handle it. You've just got to find the opening. Be smart."

Elijah nodded, opened his mouth for the mouthguard, and got to his feet. The bell rang and he moved to the centre again.

HICKS WAS in the first row, three metres away from the corner where the young man was being worked on by his trainer. His skin was slick with a light sweat, but, apart from that, there was no indication that he had been in a fight.

He had an excellent view and could see nothing that gave him any reason to think that something bad was about to happen. Ziggy had forwarded him pictures of the men who Milton had suggested might cause trouble, but he hadn't seen any of them, and they certainly were not sitting near the ring. He had shot a short video that showed the occupants of the first couple of rows and had forwarded that to Ziggy. He had explained that he would be able to run it through image-recognition software and compare it to the photographs that he had extracted from the phone Milton had stolen. No reports yet.

He heard Milton's voice in his ear. *"Anything?"*

"No," Hicks replied. "Looks normal."

"Same here," Ziggy reported. *"No positive hits."*

The referee signalled and the two fighters got to their feet. The bell rang, the referee stepped out of the way, and the two young men met in the middle of the ring.

Elijah jabbed and caught Connolly against the side of his chin, then jabbed again. He ducked and moved to his right, opened up the space between them again, then stepped forward and landed a leading right hook to the side of Connolly's head.

Hicks heard Connolly make a sound and knew that

Elijah had hurt him. Connolly shook off the effects of the punch and came on to Elijah, grabbing hold and landing short hooks into his body and around the sides of his head. Elijah tried to shake him off, but his arm was caught in Connolly's. The referee came between them, but Connolly only stepped away a couple of paces and then he was on him again.

ZIGGY WAS in Hicks's Range Rover, parked in the car park near the venue. He had taken out his laptop and set it up on the dashboard, patching it into his phone and a strong 4G signal. The laptop was showing an illegal stream of the fight while also running Ziggy's image-recognition software. The feed was processed and compared with the photographs that Ziggy had pulled from the phone that Milton had stolen. The footage concentrated on the action in the ring, but there had been several pans across the crowd before the fight had begun and during the intervals between the rounds. Hicks had also provided video from his position at the front of the crowd. There had been no hits so far, but Ziggy kept looking.

Ziggy had no interest in sport, apart from those occasions when he had broken into the websites of betting operations and manipulated the code so as to pay out to the dummy accounts he had set up. He had certainly never boxed in his life, but even he could tell that Elijah Warriner had skill.

The second round came to an end. Ziggy leaned forward, ready for the camera to cut to a wide shot, and, as it did, he heard the laptop fan spin up as the processor began to work.

There had been no hits yet, but Ziggy had worked with Milton enough to know when he was nervous, and he was nervous now. There would be a reason for that; operators like him did not scare easily.

40

McCauley squirted a jet of water over Elijah's face. Elijah blinked it out of his eyes.

"He's doing exactly as we thought," McCauley said. "He's going to try to win rounds by making it look like he's got you against the ropes and landing."

"He's not getting anything through," Elijah said breathlessly.

"Doesn't matter," McCauley replied, a smile creeping across his face. "He can't hurt you. Box with your brain. Move and throw the check hook. All right? Throw the check. He won't see it coming. You're too quick."

Elijah was up and the third round began. He walked to the centre of the ring. Connolly was into his stride, pushing him back with short punches that Elijah caught on his arms. It still forced him backwards, absorbing blows on his shoulders and forearms and gloves as he covered up on the ropes.

He was calm. He couldn't hear the noise. He was focused on Connolly and nothing else.

Connolly locked up again, then separated just enough to uncork an uppercut that blasted between Elijah's gloves and detonated on the tip of his chin. The world blurred a little and he staggered backwards. His legs felt like they weren't attached to him, and the noise around him was replaced by a high-pitched ring. He lifted his gloves up in response, an automatic reaction drilled into him by all the hours he had spent in the ring. Connolly unloaded punch after punch onto his gloves.

Elijah's senses cleared, but he was against the ropes and couldn't remember how he got there.

And then something changed.

Connolly had him in a clinch, rabbit-punching him in the kidneys. The referee left them to brawl for a moment, and then the strength seemed to ebb out of Connolly's arms. Elijah slipped the hold and saw that Connolly's guard was still down. That was strange—he had been fastidious about guarding against Elijah's power shots—but Elijah wasn't going to question the opportunity. He moved away from the ropes in one pivot and landed a check left hook as Connolly moved forward towards him again.

It stopped him in his tracks.

Elijah didn't pause to admire his work. He stepped forward and landed a double-jab, then threw a right hook that landed half on Connolly's glove and half on his chin.

Connolly staggered and Elijah pounced. He threw another right hand, then landed a left hook to the top of Connolly's jaw. He was wobbling now, sweat spraying out with every fresh impact, splashing back into Elijah's face.

Elijah came forward again, forcing Connolly against the ropes.

He landed another right hand, and suddenly Connolly was down on one knee.

Elijah was too caught up to notice, drawing back his arm

to land another punch, before the referee caught him by the bicep and moved him backwards to the neutral corner.

The noise swept over him, a barrage so abrupt it was as if someone had just turned up the volume. Elijah heard individual voices—hoarse shouts of his name, whoops of pleasure, groans of anguish—before they coalesced into one omnipresent, deafening thrum.

And it was all there in front of him. His future, his life.

Knock him down and that would be it.

The referee counted eight and let Connolly continue.

He came out to the middle of the ring. Elijah saw: Connolly couldn't focus his eyes.

Elijah unleashed a right-handed uppercut. He knew it was over as soon as it landed. He could feel the hit all the way down his arm, into his shoulder, shuddering through every single muscle along the way.

He could hear the voices again. Every noise. Every cheer.

Connolly went down as if someone had chopped him at the knees. The referee started the count. He could've gone all the way to a hundred; it wouldn't have made any difference.

Connolly was out.

PART XII

THE FIRST DAY

41

"Happy Christmas!"

Elijah was in the shower, standing under the hot jet and letting the water sluice off the sweat that had started to dry on his skin. McCauley had put his head around the door, and Elijah guessed that the clock must have ticked over to midnight.

He looked down to his feet and saw a reddening in the water, looked at his hands and saw how the knuckles had cracked and bled. He turned off the water, wrapped his towel around his waist, and went back into the dressing room.

McCauley was there, gathering up the bloody wraps and dumping them in a black bin liner with the rest of their rubbish. Elijah's shorts and boots were on the seat where he had left them. McCauley had laid out his jeans and shirt, both freshly laundered and pressed. Elijah went to the sink and looked at his reflection in the mirror.

"There's not a mark on you," McCauley observed.

"He nailed me once," Elijah disagreed, probing the side of his face.

"Don't worry. You're still pretty."

Elijah towelled himself off. His arms were sore from where Connolly had hammered at his guard, and his kidneys ached as he bent down to pull on his jeans, but that was all to be expected.

He winced as he pulled on his shirt. "What you make of Connolly?"

"Tough. We knew he would be."

"I know. But the way he went down."

"You hammered him, Mustafa."

"Yeah. Maybe. But there's something that's bothering me."

"What?"

"He had me in a clinch, right? Third round, just before I dropped him. He was bombing me inside, big hits; then he just let go. The ref didn't split us up; he just let me out."

"Maybe he thought he'd softened you up enough?"

"I don't think so. He just stood there, his guard down, like he wanted me to tag him."

McCauley reached his hand up and rested it against Elijah's cheek. "You're overthinking," he said. "You'd already tagged him—two, three big shots. I doubt he was all there by the time you put him down. Forget about it. It looked good from where I was standing."

Elijah shrugged. McCauley was probably right. There was no point in second-guessing himself. He'd done what he needed to do. He'd won the fight, sealed it with another KO that cemented his reputation as a fighter with dynamite in his fists. Elijah knew he would have looked good out there. Tommy Porter had already put his head in the door to congratulate him and to say that he needed to make sure he was at the party afterwards. He had said that there was business to discuss.

There was a knock at the door now. McCauley went over and opened it, then stepped aside.

Elijah turned. It was Alesha. He had given her a backstage pass, an embossed sticker that she was wearing on the leg of her jeans.

“Hey,” she said, a smile beaming out. “You okay?”

“I’m good,” Elijah said.

“Can I come in?” she asked.

“Course,” he said. “I’m just finishing up.”

She came inside, closing the door behind her. McCauley turned and made himself busy with the rest of the equipment.

“You looked amazing,” she said. “I was listening to what the others were saying next to me. They were saying how you were better than they thought, how you were going to be a world champion, all that. I loved it.”

She beamed at him again. He felt a buzz in his stomach, an emptiness that he usually felt when he was nervous, and he realised that the prospect of trying to get with her was scaring him more than going into the ring with someone like Connolly. She was so fine; older than him, too. He had never had much luck with women, not as a kid and not really up in Sheffield. He had been useless when he was younger, and there hadn’t been time for it since he had moved. He had been concentrating on his training for the most part. There had been a couple of things that had never gone anywhere, a little fun but nothing serious. He had never been with a girl—not properly, all the way—and the prospect of it was making him sweat.

“What are you doing now?” she asked him.

“I got the after-party,” he said, his mouth dry. “You want to come?”

“You sure?”

He nodded. "It's in Bethnal Green. Only if you can—if you're not busy, I mean."

"I'd love to," she said.

42

Milton called Sharon and asked if she knew what Elijah was planning on doing following the fight. She told him that there was a party and that she would arrange for his name to be left at the door. Milton thanked her and said that he would see her there.

He finished the call and then dialled Hicks.

"Everything okay?"

"Seems fine," Milton said.

"What's next?"

"There's a party," he said. "It'll probably be easier to get to Elijah there than it was here."

"You still worried?"

"I am."

"Where is it?"

"Bethnal Green," he said, giving Hicks the name and address that Sharon had provided for the club.

"You want me to come?"

"I'd appreciate it. His mother put me on the guest list,

but it'd be good to have someone on the outside, just in case."

"So you get to go to the party while I'm shivering in the cold?"

"You know you're going to heaven."

"I doubt that," Hicks said. *"I'll set off now. Call me if you need me."*

Milton made his way out of the Olympic Park to Stratford underground station. The Central Line ran to Bethnal Green, and he pressed himself into a busy carriage and waited for the train to set off. He wasn't ready to relax, not just yet. He had known that it would be difficult for Pinky to cause trouble at the venue, and getting to Elijah would have been almost impossible. A club was a different matter altogether. He hadn't had the chance to reconnoitre the venue, but he guessed that it would be much simpler to get inside compared to the significant security that had been put in place before the fight.

He would be much happier once the day was done and Elijah and his mother were on their way back north to Sheffield.

THE AFTER-FIGHT PARTY was at Oval Space in Bethnal Green. Elijah had never been before, but was quickly impressed. It was a large venue that was itself dominated by the disused gasholder that loomed over this part of Hackney Road. The club was situated within a large hangar; part of it had been sealed off for this event, but Elijah guessed that there would still have been more than enough space for a thousand revellers. Porter had booked it and invited all of the fighters and their entourages, together with a guest list of industry movers and shakers.

McCauley kept pace with Elijah and Alesha as they were ushered around the queue to a VIP entrance.

"Be on your best behaviour," McCauley said.

"You know me."

"I just heard. A couple of executives from HBO were over to watch the fights. You impressed them. They want to say hi."

Elijah led the way into the venue. The roof soared overhead, and the pulse and throb of bass rippled the canvas. Lasers whirled up and around, and strobes exploded over the dance floor, freezing the men and women on the floor in staccato poses.

"Mustafa!"

Elijah stopped as the promoter muscled his way through the crowd.

"Happy Christmas!" he said. "You were amazing." He turned to Alesha and put out his hand. "Tommy Porter."

"This is Alesha," Elijah said, feeling awkwardly possessive.

"Nice to meet you, Alesha. What are you three doing out here? The party's in the VIP room. Your tickets will get you in." He pointed to a roped-off area on the other side of the dance floor. "There's food and a free bar. I'll be over in a minute—see you then? We need to chat."

"See you there," McCauley said, stepping up between the two of them.

He nudged Elijah forward. Alesha reached for his hand and he gave it a squeeze.

"Be careful with him," McCauley warned. "He's as bent as a nine-bob note. If he starts talking about the next fight, tell him to come and talk to me."

"A'ight," Elijah said.

He wasn't really paying attention, not to Porter nor

McCauley. He was adrift in a delicious sensation of euphoria: the fight, the music, the softness of Alesha's skin against the calluses that had toughened up his palm.

Tonight was going to be a good night.

43

The VIP area was behind a velvet rope. They approached the bouncer who was guarding it and showed them their tickets.

The man didn't even look at them. "It's okay," he said. "I know who you are. You looked *good* tonight, son."

Elijah couldn't stop grinning. This was unreal: people he had never met before knew who he was. They respected him and what he could do.

He turned to Alesha and saw that she was smiling, too.

"Get used to it," she said. "You're prime time now."

Elijah looked around to see if his mum was here, but there was no sign of her. He thought about texting her to see where she was, but Alesha gripped his hand and dragged him to the bar.

She aimed away from it, heading towards a pair of plain double doors.

"Where are we going?" he asked her.

She turned back and smiled at him. "I've got something for you."

MILTON WALKED from Bethnal Green station to the venue. The road was busy with people enjoying a night of entertainment before the reality of Christmas set in. Groups of men and women made their way from venue to venue; Milton saw a young woman in a party dress slumped on one of the benches that lined the grassy margin of Paradise Row. He passed York Hall and thought of how much had changed for Elijah since the workout there just a few days earlier. He had done everything that he needed to do in the ring. His fate was in the hands of his trainer and promoter now. He was too young to understand the business and the politics that drove it. Milton hoped that he had surrounded himself with competent people, but then remembered Sharon; his mother was smart and wouldn't let her son be exploited. Elijah was in good hands.

He passed his hotel and kept going, turning left onto the narrow one-lane road beyond The Hare pub and continuing beneath a railway bridge as a late-running train rumbled overhead, the golden lights from the carriage casting their glow down onto the cobbles. This was an old industrial area, with warehouses and manufacturing businesses occupying the buildings that shouldered up against the banks of the Regent's Canal. He heard the thud of bass and followed the noise to a warehouse, newly refurbished, that bore a sign announcing it as Oval Space. The road was The Oval, its name derived from the island around which it split, cars parked tight up against each other atop it. There was a queue of men and women outside a flight of steps that led up, Milton presumed, to the entrance. Taxis and luxury cars fought for space along the narrow road, disgorging their passengers and then crawling away. The people were dressed in suits and cocktail dresses, many of them evidently brought here directly from the fight.

Milton continued on, scouting the street. The opulence and luxury were at odds with the surroundings: the cobbles, the derelict buildings with weeds spilling down from the roofs, the graffiti on the walls. Someone had tagged a large expanse of brick with BLACK AND WHITE UNITE—SMASH THE NATIONAL FRONT and another had added EAT THE RICH. It was new money butting hard against the area's old industrial heritage. He continued to the end of the road and a stretch of rusting iron railings that protected against the drop down to the canal. Colourful narrowboats had been moored there, lights glowing in their windows indicating that their owners were aboard. One of the boats had a Christmas tree on the roof, the branches swaying in the breeze, baubles clanking as they bumped up against each other.

Milton dialled Hicks's number, then added Ziggy to the call.

"Where are you?"

"Hit a bit of traffic," Hicks reported. *"We'll be there in fifteen minutes."*

Milton opened a map on his phone. "It's busy," Milton said. "Come off the road opposite Vyner Street, go under the bridge and park there. There's a barrier there—it's the closest you'll be able to get to the venue without getting boxed in."

"Will do. I'll let you know when we get there. What do you want us to do?"

"Stay outside and keep your eyes open."

Milton ended the call and went back to the venue.

44

Alesha didn't let go of his hand. She tugged him with her, leading the way through the VIP area, through a pair of double doors, and then into a large kitchen.

"Where we going?" he asked her again.

"Somewhere quiet," she said, smiling at him. "Can you spare ten minutes?"

"Why?"

"I want to show you how impressed I am with what you did tonight."

She pulled him on and he didn't resist. He knew what she was suggesting, and his heart quickened. The whole night had been ridiculous: the fight, the party, a girl like Alesha showing interest in him. She was *peng*—banging hot—and the thought that she would want to spend time with him was something that Elijah was struggling to get straight in his head. His mum and McCauley had told him to be careful, that there would be gold-diggers who wanted a part of him now, who might think he could make them rich or famous, but he didn't think that

Alesha was like that. She had been interested in him before tonight, before he had knocked out Connolly and guaranteed his future. Maybe she actually liked him; maybe it was time he allowed himself to think that that might be possible.

She pushed open the doors on the other side of the kitchen and led him into a corridor.

Elijah saw him, but it was too late.

Pinky.

"A'ight, JaJa?" Pinky said.

He turned back to the door. Kidz had been there, hiding against the wall, and now he was blocking the way back to the club. Elijah turned in the other direction and saw another man—Chips?—standing in an open doorway that led outside.

Pinky reached into the pocket of his padded jacket and brought out a pistol. He held it up, then lazily levelled it so that it was pointed straight into Elijah's gut. "You're coming with us."

Elijah swallowed down a gulp of fear. "No, I'm not."

Pinky lurched at Elijah, bringing the butt of the pistol across his cheek. The metal clashed against his cheekbone, and, with his head ringing, he reached up and saw fresh blood on his fingertips.

Pinky took his advantage, pressing the gun against Elijah's head. "I'll do you now, right here, you diss me again. Don't fuck me around, blood. You're coming outside with us."

He felt the swoon of dizziness, leaned down and spat out a mouthful of blood onto the floor. There was a flash of white amid the red. It was funny, and he almost laughed at the foolishness of it: he'd been in the ring with Connolly, but it was now, afterwards, that a tooth had been knocked out. He put out his hand and supported himself against the wall of the corridor.

He looked back for Alesha. He didn't know what to say, whether he should tell Pinky to leave her alone or just say nothing and hope that whatever it was he was going to do, he would do it and forget about her. His concern curdled when he saw her face.

"What?" she said, her arms spread. The warm smile and the playful tone in her voice were gone.

"What's going on?" he said through a bloodied mouth.

"Payback," she replied.

"What?"

"You gonna pay for what you did. For what you took from me. From me and my family."

She stepped forward and spat in his face. He wiped it away, his fingers covered with commingled blood and saliva.

Pinky grabbed him by the collar and yanked, sending him towards the open door. He followed close behind, and Elijah could feel the muzzle of the pistol in the small of his back. They exited the building and made their way around a narrow passage between the wall on the left and a wooden fence on the right. The venue butted up against a larger square building, and to Elijah the path looked like a dead end. He was almost sick with the fear that he was going to be put up against the wall and shot. But it wasn't a dead end; there was a gate in the fence and Chips opened it, leading the way into a space between the buildings that had been used to park cars.

One of the cars had its engine running, its headlights glowing against the side of the building opposite. The lid of the boot was open.

Pinky kicked him on the backside. "In."

Elijah went to the car and turned around, his eyes on the

tiny black hole in the muzzle of the pistol, his mind spooling up his memories of Pinky, of what he had been capable of as a boy.

"Get in the car, JaJa. I don't wanna ask you again."

Elijah hooked his leg over the lip of the boot and hopped up, lying flat and drawing his knees up to his chest.

Pinky and Alesha stepped up to the back of the car, looking down at him.

"You gonna get *proper* dooked, bro," Pinky said, grinning at him.

The boot slammed shut.

45

Milton ignored the grumbles of those waiting in the queue as he made his way up the stairs to the front of the line and told the bouncer that his name had been left at the door. The man grunted, nodding to a woman with a clipboard who was standing by a smaller, secondary door.

"My name is Milton," he said. "I should be on the list."

She ran her finger down a piece of paper until she found his name. "There you are," she said. "In you go."

The venue was large. The room had been cordoned off halfway down its length, but it was still a big space. There was a dance floor, a DJ booth and several bars. A projector hung down from a scaffold, and it was projecting the bouts onto a large screen. Milton looked up to see a ten-foot-tall Elijah covering up and then uncorking the big uppercut that had nearly knocked Connolly out of his boots.

Milton heard Ziggy's voice in his ear. *"Milton—you there?"*

"I'm inside," he said. "What is it?"

"I got a hit."

Milton felt a shiver pass down his back; he found a corridor and made his way through a pair of double doors and into the gents, the sound of the PA fading just a little. "Go on."

"You sent me a picture—a girl coming out of the dressing room? I only just got it."

"I sent it two hours ago—"

"There was limited capacity in the park. Look—it doesn't matter. You need to know this. You know the girl?"

"I don't know anything save that I think she's involved with Elijah."

"Her name's Tiffany Brown. Currently unemployed, but was taking a media degree before she was expelled six months ago. She was interning at Vice, but something happened and they sent her back. She has a criminal record for wounding, theft and possession. She's also the sister of Solomon Brown and Israel Brown—"

"Oh shit," Milton said. "Oh *shit*."

He turned back, pushed the door, and went back out into the noise of the club.

"Milton—you still there?"

Milton scoured left and right, looking for Elijah.

"Milton?"

"I'm here," he said, only half listening.

"Israel Brown was the real name of Risky Bizness, shot dead in Hackney three years ago. Solomon Brown is Tiffany's older brother. He's never been convicted of anything, but the Met police have a file on him as long as your arm. He's suspected of running a local drugs syndicate, and he's been implicated in at least three murders. He's—"

Milton saw Sharon. He ended the call and intercepted her on her way to the bathroom.

"Hi, John," she said with a wide, happy smile. "Are you okay?"

"I'm fine," he said, working hard to keep the edge of panic from his voice. "Have you seen Elijah?"

"He was in the VIP room," she said. "Why? Is everything okay?"

"Yes," he said, forcing out a smile of his own. "I just wanted to check up on him. Where is it?"

She pointed behind her. "Over there. What's up?"

"Nothing," he said.

"I mentioned you were there tonight. He said to say thanks."

Milton wanted to get over to the room, to check that Elijah was okay, but he didn't want to frighten Sharon unnecessarily, either. "That's great," he said, starting to move to the side so that he could get around her.

She reached out and took his elbow. "He asked if you'd like to see him tomorrow. I think he wants to apologise."

"I'd love to," he said, gently removing her hand and sliding around her. "Tell him that'd be great. I'm just going to the bar. I'll see you in a minute."

He walked away from her before she could stop him. He dialled Hicks again, the call connecting as he circumnavigated the dance floor.

"Yes?" Hicks said.

"Where are you?"

"Outside," he said.

"Have you seen anyone leave?"

"There's a crowd here. Who are you looking for?"

"Elijah. He might be with a woman—black, mid-twenties, pretty."

"Ziggy sent me her picture," Hicks said. *"I haven't seen her. Not out the front, anyway."*

"They won't go out the front." He opened the map on his phone. The club was bordered to the east by the patch of land with the derelict gasholders and to the south by the canal. There was no way out by car in either direction. The main entrance was to the west and would be too busy. If they could get out to the north, they could get onto Hackney Road and be gone. "Go north," he said. "Up to Emma Street."

Milton reached the private area. A large bouncer was guarding the entrance, his hand resting around the end of a velvet rope that was strung between two chrome poles. The VIP room was around a short corner, and Milton couldn't see inside it from where he was standing.

"You can't come in here," the man said.

"I need to go through," he insisted.

"And I told you that you can't. Step back, please, sir."

Milton took a step back, watched the man's posture loosen, and then drilled him in the face with a straight right. The man was big, but his chin was soft; he staggered back, the rope catching around him as he fell down to his backside, both poles clattering into his lap. Milton knew that he had a limited window; the other bouncers would be called over.

It didn't matter: he had to make sure that Elijah was safe.

Milton made his way into the VIP room. He took it in, appraising it quickly and professionally: thirty guests, two members of staff with canapés, a bar with a bartender working behind it. He could see Elijah's trainer and the young promoter, Porter.

He couldn't see Elijah.

He heard the sound of a commotion behind him and knew that he didn't have long before the security arrived to take him out. He stepped forward, between the trainer and Porter.

"Excuse me," he said.

The trainer frowned. "Who are you?"

"A friend of Elijah."

"Elijah?"

Milton gritted his teeth in frustration. "Sorry—Mustafa. Do you know where he is?"

"I don't know you. How do you know him?"

"Milton," Hicks said, *"there's a yard on the other side of the building. There was a car, lights on."*

Fuck.

"Can you stop it?"

"What?" the trainer said, thinking Milton was talking to him.

"It's gone," Hicks said. *"Headed west on Emma Street, then left, up to Hackney Road. What do you want me to do?"*

"Can you follow it?"

"Ziggy's only just brought the car around."

The trainer rested a hand on Milton's shoulder. "Excuse me?"

He turned back to the man. He was frowning, evidently confused by Milton's behaviour.

"Who are you?" the trainer said.

"I'm a friend of Mustafa's mother. Just wanted to say congratulations to him. Do you know where he is?"

"He was here. Last I saw him he was over by the bar."

"Thank you."

Milton went to the bar and saw the door to the side of it. He knew what had happened.

"Wait for me down there," he said to Hicks.

"Copy that."

Milton opened the double doors and went through into the kitchen beyond. It was empty. Milton moved inside and, as he did, a second set of doors opened on the other side of the room.

A woman came through them.

46

Milton ducked down behind the stainless-steel counter. It was the girl: Tiffany Brown. She was on her phone and distracted. Milton had been shielded by a tall set of shelves that held pots and pans; she hadn't seen him.

"It's done," she said. "Nah—easy. He had no idea, man. The kid put him in the car. They'll be there soon." She paused, leaning back against the counter on the other side of where Milton was hiding. "I know—gonna be a nice Christmas present. Love you, bruv."

It was quiet as she ended the call. Milton waited for her to walk around the counter and then moved, much too fast for her to do anything about it. He raised himself up, slipped an arm around her slender body, and clamped his hand over her mouth. He wrapped the other arm around her, too, and then dragged her back to the door through which she had entered the room.

"Not a sound," he whispered into her ear as he dragged her, one of her heels falling off her foot.

She was light, but, as Milton forced her through the door, she fought back. She wriggled and tried to scrape her remaining heel down his shin; the point of the heel was sharp, and it gouged a scratch through his trouser leg. Milton tightened his grip, holding her still, but she didn't give up. She forced her head up and, before Milton could stop her, she bit down on his index finger. Pain shot up his arm; his grip loosened and she slid out of his grasp.

He was in the way, preventing her from making her way back to the club. She backed away and, before Milton could get to her, she let out an ear-splitting scream. The music was loud in the club, and he doubted that anyone would hear, but Milton was left with no choice; he closed in and, as she raked her nails up at his face, he swept her hand away and then punched her flush in the face.

She staggered backwards, dazed, and Milton moved to take advantage. He hoisted her up into a fireman's carry, wrapping his right arm around her torso to pin her left arm and angling her so that her right arm was trapped against his shoulder. He was able to manhandle her easily through the door and into the corridor beyond. It was lit by a strip light, and there was enough light for him to see the blood on the floor. He felt the familiar twinge of anger, the buzz of violence, his darker nature shucking off its shackles and baring its teeth, and concentrated on keeping it tamped down so that he could do what he had to do.

There was a door to the outside and a passage beyond that. Milton carried the woman to the end of the passage and the open gate into the yard beyond. Hicks's Range Rover was parked there, backed in, the rear lights glowing blood red. Milton hurried, opening the door and dumping the woman inside and over the seats. He got in next to her and closed the door. Hicks was in the passenger seat, and Ziggy was driving.

"Go," Milton said.

47

Elijah had his knees drawn up to his chest with no space to move. He was lying on his right shoulder and, as the car continued on its journey, he started to feel the first painful stabs of cramp. His face was sore from where Pinky had pistol-whipped him. With his tongue, he probed the gap where the tooth had been knocked out, the taste of blood lingering in his mouth.

It was completely dark and he could hear the sound of the tyres against the surface of the road. He occasionally thought he heard muffled conversation and then a gale of what was unmistakably laughter.

He knew that he was in trouble.

Pinky had always been frightening. Elijah remembered him from the years he had spent on the estate. He'd had a bad reputation; Elijah had heard stories that Pinky used to entertain himself by shooting the neighbourhood cats with his air rifle. The recollection of that stirred another memory that he had long since buried; he remembered watching the video that Pinky had taken of himself stealing a dog from one of the old women who lived in the sheltered accommodation around the corner from Blissett House. He had used a kitchen knife to cut the dog's throat. Pinky had posted it on YouTube; Elijah remembered the snicker of his laughter behind the camera as the animal had choked on its own blood.

And Elijah's mum had grassed Pinky up to the police. What happened next was talked about incessantly at school: Pinky had been arrested and taken to the police station for questioning. His mother had been disgusted with him and had threatened to kick him out of the house if he didn't change his ways. Pinky was a proud boy, and Elijah had known that it would have cut him up to know that the kids at school were laughing at him. Elijah's mum had suggested shortly afterwards that they should move away from the city —away from the temptations that had so nearly ruined his life—and he had been glad to find that he agreed with her.

He hadn't expected to see Pinky ever again.

It seemed he had been wrong about that, and the consequences could only be bad.

The car continued. Elijah found it difficult to gauge how long they had been travelling, and had no idea at all where they were. The car slowed down and he felt the rattle and bump as the wheels passed over rough ground. The engine idled and then was switched off.

The cramping was really bad now, throbbing in his shoulder and in both thighs. He heard the sound of doors opening and closing, and then footsteps crunching across uneven ground.

The lid of the boot opened, and artificial light shone inside. It was a torch; Elijah looked away.

"Get out," said Pinky.

Elijah sat up, wincing from the sudden aches and pains that were stirred by his movement. Hands reached for him, two pairs, and Elijah saw that Kidz was there, too. He and Pinky dragged him out of the boot and dumped him on the ground next to the back of the car. He was on his hands and knees and could smell the fumes from the exhaust. He glanced around. The car had been parked on a patch of rough ground with a row of garages on either side and a track leading into what looked like a council estate. He could hear the sound of passing cars on a major road nearby, but there was nothing else to tell him where they might be. The sky above was dark, a vault of cloud obscuring the moon and stars. The only light was from the torch and the glow of the car's lights. Snow was falling.

He saw Pinky take a run up but wasn't able to defend himself as he booted him in the ribs. The impact was sudden and shocking, punching the air out of his lungs and blasting a sharp pain up and down his body. He slumped to the ground, his cheek scraping against pebbles and stones.

"Get him up."

Kidz was on one side and Chips was on the other. They grabbed him, hauling him onto his feet. He looked up: the garages looked as if they were derelict and unused, save for one that leaked a little light from a crack between its double doors.

"Where are we?" Elijah said.

"Somewhere no one will be able to find you," Pinky said.

"Why?"

"Friend of mine wants to meet you," he said.

48

Pinky led the way with the other two half-carrying, half-dragging Elijah across the rough ground. He went up to the garage and opened the doors, letting more of the light spill outside. Elijah looked up as they marched him inside. The garage was dilapidated, with leaks in the roof that had allowed pools of rainwater to gather on the floor and lichen growing up the walls. It was larger than he had expected, and looked as if two garages had been knocked together to form a bigger space. Two-thirds of the interior had been given over to what Elijah could see was a sophisticated cannabis farm. The garage had been converted for a hydroponic set-up, with electrical cables snaking down from the ceiling to a series of powerful overhead lights and an elaborate irrigation system. Ducted air-conditioning units had been installed, the motors whirring constantly, with plastic sheeting separating the farm from the remaining third of the space. That part was empty, save for a wooden chair that had been placed beneath the single bulb that hung overhead.

Elijah was taken to the chair and forced onto it. Kidz

went over to a table and picked up a handful of cable ties. Chips took Elijah by the left elbow and wrist and held his arm against the arm of the chair; Kidz looped two of the ties around his arm and zipped them up until they were tight. They repeated the trick with Elijah's right arm. He didn't struggle; there were three of them, and Pinky had a gun. What would have been the point?

"Come on," Elijah protested. "You don't need to do this."

A radio was playing on a bench at the side of the room; he could hear an old Christmas song: 'Jingle Bell Rock.' He noticed Kidz looking over to the cannabis farm and followed his eye. He could see the outline of a man through the translucent plastic sheeting; two sheets were parted and the man stepped into the light. He was black, tall, and had a well-trimmed beard. He was wearing a black Adidas tracksuit top, a pair of Levi's and pristine white trainers.

"Hello," the man said.

"Who are you?"

"I'm Sol," he said. "What do you prefer? Elijah or Mustafa?"

"Elijah," he said.

"You're a pretty shit Muslim, blood," the man said, grinning. He had a gold tooth; it glittered in the light.

"I don't know who you are," Elijah said.

"Nah," the man replied. "I stay under the radar. My brother was different—you know Bizness, right?"

Elijah swallowed down a mouthful of bilious fear.

"Yeah," Sol said, "I see you do. He was always all about getting props for himself, always wanted to be famous, right from when he was a younger hanging around the blocks. Never saw the point in it myself. The kind of business we do, it don't make too much sense to draw attention to yourself.

Israel was a good rapper, right, but as a businessman?" Sol sucked his teeth. "Man was poor."

The song on the radio faded out and was replaced with another. Sol paused, cocking his head, and then grinned. "'Blue Christmas,'" he said. "You like Elvis?"

Elijah didn't know what to say. "I suppose."

"Nah," he said. "White man pretending to be black. I studied that shit at school. Been happening since time began. Still happening today. Your promoter—he's a white boy, right? I seen him on the TV."

"Yeah," Elijah said.

"You ask me, you need to work with another brother. I'm from these ends, too. Just like you."

Elijah flexed his arms, felt the plastic cable ties pull tight against his flesh. There was no give there.

Sol noticed. "I'll let you out in a minute," he said. "Once I've said my piece, you can show me that I can trust you."

"What do you want?"

"First up? I want to tell you about me. I'm a professional, Elijah. I'm all about making my Ps." He pointed at the farm. "You see that? Two hundred cannabis plants, right there. The unit next to this one is a drying room. We got another unit with mature plants, ready to be cropped. I own all of these garages. Paid fifty grand for them last year. Made that last week. We grow a lot of dope here, make a lot of money."

He moved closer to where Pinky was standing and put an arm around his shoulders. "My boy Shaquille, here, he's all for taking a knife to your pretty face. That right, younger?"

Elijah knew that Pinky hated his given name; he saw him stiffen from the use of it, and then the derogative reference to his status.

"That's what we agreed," Pinky said through gritted

teeth. "I bring him; then we teach him not to diss us. You said we was gonna shank him. That's what—"

"Hush your gums," Sol snapped.

"Sol?"

The man turned and cuffed Pinky across the face with the back of his hand. "What's wrong with you, younger? You forget your place? Shut the fuck up or we're going to have a beef."

Sol turned back to Elijah, dismissing Pinky with a flick of his wrist. "I ain't a barbarian. No one's shanking anyone. I want to talk to you about a business proposition. You know I helped you tonight, right?"

Elijah saw the way Pinky was looking at the older man and knew that things were about to get much, much worse.

"Come on," Sol was saying. "You didn't notice? Connolly went down because I told him to go down. I made good money on that fight, but the way I see it, that's just a starter. I want mad money out of you, Elijah, no pocket change. That's what we gonna talk about. You and me, blood—we're going to go into business together."

Sol was compelling, and frightening, but Elijah couldn't take his eyes off Pinky. He was behind Sol, staring at him, his eyes burning with hate and anger. Elijah watched as Pinky reached into his pocket. His eyes flashed with hot enmity, and his lips were pulled back to show his white teeth clenched together in an ugly grin of anticipation.

"Don't," Elijah said to him.

Sol turned around.

49

Hicks drove them out of Bethnal Green and deeper into East London. They had changed drivers so that Ziggy could work on finding Elijah. The young man's phone was dead, so Ziggy had started to excavate the data from Tiffany's phone instead. The device was locked, but it was equipped with a fingerprint scanner, and Milton held the girl's finger over it until the screen came to life. Ziggy plugged it into his laptop and set to work, his fingers flashing across the keyboard, information scrolling quickly down the screen.

Milton had secured the girl's wrists with a length of rope that Hicks kept in the back of the car and, to forestall any possibility of her screams, he had balled up a chamois leather and pushed it into her mouth. She had decided that it was pointless to resist and, for the last ten minutes, she had stared out of the window, occasionally glaring at him in the reflection in the glass. Milton didn't care about that. She had conspired in the plot to kidnap Elijah, and he would give her reason to be sullen if she didn't help them fix the mess that she had helped create.

"They're in Woodford," Ziggy said.

"Are you sure?"

"Yes. They both have Android, and they've given each other Trusted Contact status. His phone shares its position with hers."

"Where in Woodford?"

"Look."

Ziggy held his laptop so that Milton could see the Google Map on the screen. A blue dot was dead centre of a residential district. Ziggy switched to a satellite image and zoomed in: Milton saw the curve of the M11, the oval of a running track, playing fields and a grid of streets. The dot was hovering over a small area of cleared ground in the middle of the housing estate.

"It's garages," Ziggy said. "Lock-ups. Here."

He clicked across to another screen that showed a listing on Gumtree. It was titled 'Garage for rent, north London next to M11, storage/eBay/goods/etc.' and a series of nine pictures showed an almost derelict line of garages with houses visible behind them.

"Is this recent?" Milton asked.

"A year ago."

"How long to get there?"

"Thirty minutes," Hicks said. "It's Christmas. The roads are clear."

"Faster," Milton said, and exhaled impatiently as Hicks pressed down on the accelerator.

Milton looked out of the window. They were on the A12 and had just crossed the River Lea. The area on either side of the dual carriageway was industrial, and, given the hour, it was quiet.

Time to talk to the girl.

She was still staring out of the window.

"I'm going to take out your gag," Milton told her.

She glared at him.

Milton took out the chamois.

She stared at him with icy, frigid eyes.

"I know who you are," Milton said.

"Yeah?"

"You're Tiffany Brown."

"Big whoop," she said.

"Do you know who I am?"

Doubt flickered across her face, but she brazened it out. She shrugged. "You ain't the police."

"No," he said. "I'm not—but you might wish that I was. My name is John."

"Nah," she said, dredging up some bravado. "Don't know no Johns."

"I killed your brother. That help?"

He watched her face: confusion became anger, which then deformed into fury. She lurched across the cabin in an attempt to get at him, forgetting that her hands were secured and overbalancing, falling onto the seat between them. Milton grabbed her collar and levered her back to a sitting position.

She spat at him. Milton wiped it from his cheek.

"Finished?" he said.

"You're a dead man."

"Not tonight."

She looked ready to fire back, but, instead, she breathed out sharply and looked away.

"You've got a choice," Milton told her. "The easier way out of this is to help us. What happens next to you and your brother won't be nearly as bad as it will be if you don't."

"I ain't scared of you, battyman."

"You should be. I've got everything on your phone. My friend in the front"—he nodded to Ziggy—"has already downloaded everything on it. Shall I ask him to tell you what he's found out so far?"

She clenched her jaw so tightly that Milton could see the tendons knotting in her neck.

"Ziggy?"

"We know about Solomon," Ziggy said. "We know you've been plotting with him to kidnap Elijah. You've not been very careful with your texting. Lots of evidence that the police will be interested in seeing if anything happens to him."

She shrugged. "You're bluffing. There ain't no messages."

Milton sighed. He didn't want to play his hand, but she hadn't given him much of a choice.

"We know you have a daughter," Ziggy said. "Violet."

"You son of a—"

"She's with your parents tonight," Ziggy said. "And I know where they live."

"You threatening my girl?"

"No," Milton said. "I'd never hurt a child. But she's going to grow up without a mother if you don't help me. No one will ever see you again. You will just disappear."

She laughed, but it was nervous and uncertain. "You're bluffing," she repeated, but with less conviction than the first time.

"Your brother thought I was bluffing," Milton said.

Her eyes burned with fury, and Milton could see that she would like nothing more than to dig her long painted nails into his face. That wasn't going to happen, though; she was helpless, and Milton knew that he was convincing. He had meant it, too. If anything happened to Elijah, he would punish her and her brother. He would burn through them both. She was angry, but she wasn't stupid.

When she spoke again, her voice was quieter. "What do you want?"

"We know where they are," Milton said. "I want you to tell me what we'll find when we get there."

50

Pinky could still feel the sting of the slap from where Sol had struck him. His cheek was hot, not from the impact, but from the blood that had rushed up to suffuse it. He felt the rush of anger, so fast and so powerful that there was nothing he could do to slow it down. It was as if he were lifted out of his body, looking down at himself as Sol turned away from him and went to stand in front of JaJa. The anger pulsed and throbbed and pounded, and he clenched his teeth together so hard that they ached. He reached his hand into his jacket pocket.

"Don't," Elijah said.

Too late for that, Pinky thought.

Sol turned around just as Pinky raised the pistol.

"What are you doing?" Sol said, looking down at it.

"You and your brother, you're just the same."

Sol smiled at him as if he still could not, not even now—not even with a nine pointed at his gut—think to take him seriously. "Put it down, Pinky."

The anger rolled over him, impossible to stop. "He treated me like I was nothing, like I was worse than nothing, just someone he could tell what to do. You're the same. Well, fuck that, Sol. Fuck *that* and fuck *you*."

There must have been something in his expression that gave him away, because now—but too late—Sol lifted his arms, palms out, a gesture of supplication. Pinky was consumed by the fury, all of the old slights and disparagements running through his head like a video playing at ten times speed. He pulled the trigger and the gun barked, the recoil kicking against his hand. Sol was close and Pinky had spent hours practising his shooting; there was no possibility that he might miss. The bullet landed square in Sol's chest, slamming into his sternum. He took a step back, his balance disturbed by the swat of the impact, and then looked down at the blood that was already saturating the tracksuit top that he was wearing. He looked back up at Pinky, frowning, his mouth opening and closing as if he was trying—and failing—to find the words that he wanted to say.

Pinky was overcome by rage and disgust and hatred. He stepped closer and pulled the trigger again, then took another step and pulled it for a third time.

"Pinky!"

He wheeled around, following the sound of the panicked voice, the gun finding Kidz, freezing him to the spot.

"What are you doing, man?" Kidz said, his hands jerking up as he stepped back.

The anger dissipated, but it left something in its wake: there was a peacefulness, a sense of calm. Pinky found that he was breathing quickly, but that was all. *Shooting someone dead? It ain't no thing*, he thought. His hands were steady and he wasn't shaking.

"You shot him!" Kidz said.

"Yeah," he said. "I did. So?"

"That's Sol, man. Jesus! It's Solomon fucking Brown."

"I don't care who he is. Man's still gonna bleed when he gets shot, right? He's just the same as me and you."

Pinky looked down. Sol was on the floor, his hands fluttering over his chest, blood draining out of the trio of holes that the bullets had made.

Kidz started to back away. Pinky looked over at him and shook his head. "Where you going, blood?"

"Nowhere, man. I ain't going nowhere."

"S'right. You staying right there where I can see you."

Pinky walked forward, stepped around Sol's body, and went over to Elijah, who was staring up at him, his eyes bulging. Pinky winked at him.

"That ain't the first time I pulled a trigger. You know that? You know who I topped before?"

"Pops," Elijah said.

"That's right." Pinky looked down at him. "You know that? I know you and him were tight, but he was just the same, just like Sol. Never gave me credit. Always talking down to me like I was this piece of *shit* on his creps."

There was a clamour as someone opened the door. Pinky turned as Chips came inside the lock-up.

"What's going on?" he said. "I heard..." The words trailed off.

"Come in and shut the door," Pinky said.

Chips saw the body on the floor. "What the fuck, man?"

Chips and Kidz exchanged a glance. Pinky could see how frightened the two of them were. He loved it.

"What have you done?"

"Yeah," he said. "Him, Pops—they think they're special, that they're badmen, but they ain't. They ain't nothing. And now they're both dead."

Pinky could feel his anger rising again, flames flickering

across the tinder of all the humiliations and indignities that he had suffered throughout his life. Growing up with no dad. His mum bringing home a new man every Friday night. The men who hit him, who hit his mum. The jokes that he heard in the playground. Never respected, never taken seriously.

"What the fuck, man?" Chips said. "What's the *matter* with you?"

No respect, not even now.

Pinky turned, aimed at Chips, and pulled the trigger again. Chips went down, dead before he hit the floor, a neat hole drilled in the centre of his forehead. It was even easier this time. Kidz gasped, but fear had nailed him to the spot, and he hadn't taken a step before Pinky swivelled, aimed, and fired again.

Two minutes, three dead men.

Easy.

Pinky turned back to Elijah. "Just me and you now," he said. He stepped a little closer. "You all right?"

Elijah gaped at him, his eyes white.

"Still think you're a big shot?"

Elijah mumbled something.

Pinky reached down and rested the gun against his head. "What's that?"

"No," Elijah said. "I don't."

"Good—you're not. You heard Sol. Your boy tonight—Sol and me paid him a visit the other day and persuaded him to go down in the third. So don't be thinking that everything they're saying about you is true. He put out his chin and you hit it. That's all you did. You ain't nothing. You never were."

51

Elijah felt the gun against his head. The barrel was hot and he could feel it burning him, but he closed his eyes and did his best to ignore the pain. He tried not to think about what Pinky had just done, how easily, almost reflexively, he had aimed the pistol and pulled the trigger. Each pull seemed easier than the last. Three dead men lay on the floor. He didn't know Sol, but he had grown up with Chips and Kidz. Pinky had grown up with them, too, and he had dispatched them without a second's thought. Elijah knew that Pinky would do the same to him.

"What do you want?" he said, his voice cracking.

"Sol wanted to make some bread off you, but I don't care about that. I remember what you did before you and your mum disappeared. She called the po-po on me, man. I know you know that. They came and arrested me in my mum's house. You know how that made her feel? The neighbours was watching when they took me out. They had me in cuffs. She didn't speak to me for a week. Said I'd embarrassed her in front of all her friends."

"I'm sorry about that," Elijah said.

"You *gonna* be sorry," Pinky said, laughing. "I ain't like Sol. I ain't like his brother. I don't care about money. I want *respect*. I want people to look at me and think there ain't no way they want to mess with me. I want people to cross over the road when they see me coming. I want them to piss their pants when I come around. People gonna know that I shot those three. And people gonna know that I dooked you, too. But I ain't using a strap for that." He reached into his pocket and took out a butterfly knife. He flicked his wrist and the blade snapped out. "A strap's too good for a pussy like you. You and me, JaJa, we gonna spend some time together first."

Pinky grabbed hold of Elijah's chin and forced his head back, exposing his throat. He leaned closer. Elijah felt the cold of the blade against his skin.

Pinky laughed. "One slice, blood, and you're *done*."

Elijah thought he saw movement behind Pinky. It was the door. He thought that it had opened, but it was a miniscule movement, so slight that he discounted it as a trick of the light.

And then it moved again.

"I didn't mean to diss you," Elijah said.

"Too late for that."

"I didn't ask my mum to call the police."

"But she did. Now she's gonna have to bury her boy because of it. I heard about your brother. She's gonna bury both her kids."

The door opened slowly, and, as Elijah watched, he saw a figure slide through it, merging into the shadows. It was gloomy over there and Pinky was partially blocking the way; he couldn't see who it was.

"Come on, man," Elijah said. "I said I'm sorry. You don't need to do this."

The figure slipped out of the shadows, moving silently,

passing from the gloom and into the fringe of the light thrown down by the single naked bulb.

It was Milton.

Elijah tried to keep his face neutral, but the surprise and the hope must have been written across it. Pinky looked down at Elijah and frowned. He spun around. Milton was halfway between the door and the chair.

Still too far away.

Pinky dropped the knife, shoved his hand into his jacket, and yanked out the gun, the frame catching against the pocket. Milton came forward, but it was too late; Pinky had the gun aimed at him and Milton froze.

"Put the gun down, Shaquille."

"This gets better and better," Pinky said. "I get you, too, old man."

Milton looked beyond Pinky to the three dead bodies strewn around the lock-up.

"This isn't going to end the way you want it to."

Pinky's rage detonated. "Shut the fuck up! I had it up to here with people telling me what I can and can't do. You blind, blood? You ain't seeing this?" He proffered the gun. "You see who's got the strap and who ain't? You don't get to tell me shit. You get to beg for your life."

Pinky had unconsciously taken a step back, moving away from Milton. He was closer to Elijah. Close enough, perhaps. Elijah looked across the room, caught Milton's attention, and held his gaze. Milton saw him, but didn't react. Elijah hoped he knew what he was going to try to do.

Pinky aimed.

Elijah kicked, his right leg straightening all the way out, just enough for his foot to butt up against the back of Pinky's right knee. Pinky's leg folded inwards, his right shoulder dipped, and his arm jerked out to the right at the moment he pulled the trigger.

The round missed, cracking into the door, wood chips and brick dust punched out.

Milton moved, lunging ahead, closing the distance between himself and Pinky in three steps, fast enough that Pinky didn't have time to aim again. Milton locked his left hand around Pinky's right wrist and then turned around, maintaining the grip so that he had his right shoulder beneath Pinky's right elbow. He took Pinky's wrist in both hands, twisted the arm so that it was elbow down, and then wrenched on it. Pinky screamed as the joint hyperextended and then dislocated; Elijah heard it pop as the elbow pushed and rotated out of its socket.

The gun fired again, the round cracking into the brick wall.

Milton held onto Pinky's wrist with his left hand and reached for the gun with his right. He took it out easily, tossing it to the side. Elijah watched with a mixture of relief and horror as Milton backed into Pinky's body, reached up over his head to grab the back of Pinky's jacket with his left hand, and then pivoted at the same time as he yanked. Pinky flipped over Milton's shoulder and landed on his back. Milton stepped to his left, pivoted and then fell onto Pinky, a knee on either side of his torso, pinning his arms to his sides. Milton leaned forward and closed his hands around Pinky's throat and squeezed.

Pinky was younger than Milton, but Milton was heavier and stronger and, as Elijah watched with mounting dread, it was evident that this was something that he had done before.

Pinky started to choke.

"Don't," Elijah said.

Milton ignored him.

"Please," he said. "Don't. There's been enough of that."

Milton's face was a mask: impassive, resolute, his eyes icy blue and without life or feeling.

"*Please*, John. Don't."

Milton's face flickered with indecision. He held on for a moment more, then released his hands from Pinky's throat and straightened up. He leaned back.

Elijah exhaled.

Pinky's right arm was disabled, lying loose at his side, the forearm bent at an unnatural angle from where Milton had dislocated it. His left hand flashed up, clutching the butterfly knife that he had discarded earlier. Elijah guessed: Pinky must have fallen on it when Milton had put him to the floor.

Pinky stabbed out with the blade, the point scoring across the back of Milton's hand as he raised it, deflecting it from his throat. Instead, the knife landed in Milton's shoulder. Pinky tried to pull it out so that he could stab again, but Milton reached up with his left hand, grabbed Pinky's hand, and held it there, the blade still lodged where it was. He leaned out, scooped up the discarded pistol, put the muzzle against the side of Pinky's head and fired.

The blast echoed back from the arched ceiling and bounced off the walls. A spray of blood and brain scattered out, splattering across the brick. Pinky's legs twitched once and then twice, and then he lay still. His fingers slithered off the knife and his arm flopped down.

The door opened and a second man, one whom Elijah did not recognise, came inside.

Milton pulled the blade out of his shoulder.

The radio changed. Bing Crosby's version of 'Little Drummer Boy' started playing.

"Ziggy says the police are coming," the second man said. "We need to go."

Milton gestured over at Elijah. "Untie him."

The man came over to the chair and, using the knife that Milton had been stabbed with, sliced through the cable ties that had fastened his wrists to the arms of the chair.

Milton had found a rag and was holding it to his shoulder.

"Are you okay?" Elijah asked him.

"I'm fine." He glanced over at Pinky's body. "I'm sorry."

Elijah felt tears in his eyes; he didn't know what to say.

"We need to go," the newcomer said again.

"You need to come with us," Milton said to him. "You don't want them to find you here."

Elijah nodded. He was confused, and the outburst of violence had been as horrifying as it had been sudden, and he knew that he had to reach out for something. He trusted Milton and realised now that he should always have trusted him. He looked at the man, the rag already reddening with blood that had been spilt on his behalf, and he felt foolish for ever doubting him.

The second man opened the door and they stepped outside. Snow was falling: huge, fat flakes that spiralled down from the blackness, twisting and twirling as they dropped through the golden glow of headlamps from the Range Rover that was parked on the patch of rough ground in front of the garages. The snow was settling; a white covering already lay atop the corrugated roofs of the garages. Elijah allowed himself to be led to the car. He saw that there were two people inside.

The second man opened the door, reached into the back and dragged out one of those people.

It was Alesha.

She tripped and fell to her knees in the snow. Her hands were secured behind her back, but the second man released them.

"She's not who she said she was," Milton said.

"Who is she?"

"Tiffany Brown. She's Solomon and Israel Brown's sister."

Alesha looked up at him, defiant and full of rage, but Elijah ignored her. There was nothing to say. Her thirst for vengeance had led her here: abandoned and about to discover the body of a second dead brother. Elijah had no sympathy for her. He felt nothing at all.

"Let's go," Milton said.

Elijah got into the back seat. There was a man in the driver's seat, and police radio played from a laptop that had been placed on the dashboard. Milton got in next to him, and the second man pulled himself into the front passenger seat. The driver started the engine and they pulled away. Elijah looked back and saw Alesha as she stumbled towards the open garage door.

She screamed.

Elijah heard the sound of sirens in the distance. The snow started to fall more heavily now, the wipers scraping it off the windshield.

The car slowly accelerated away.

EPILOGUE

Milton made his way down the aisle to the bathroom at the back of the coach. He unbuttoned his shirt and took it off, hanging it from the hook on the back of the door. The coach swept around a corner, and Milton put out his hand to brace himself; he winced in discomfort, his shoulder aching from the effort.

The bathroom was small, with just enough room for him to stand in front of the sink. He looked into the mirror and peeled off the dressing. Hicks had stitched up the wound. Pinky's blade had sliced into his muscle, its progress halted as it had butted up against his scapula. There had been a fair amount of blood, but Milton had been fortunate; it was a flesh wound, not particularly deep, and it had missed anything that might have made it more complicated to fix. Milton had been confident that he would be able to treat it himself. Ziggy had found a pharmacist that was open, and he had somehow faked a prescription for antibiotics. Milton had collected it on his way to the coach station.

The wound had been neatly stitched with a surgeon's

knot, sealing the two edges of the incision. Milton pressed gently on it and a little fluid leaked out between the sutures. Milton unwrapped an antiseptic wipe and cleaned the wound, then applied a fresh dressing. He cleaned up, put his shirt on and buttoned it up, and went back outside.

THERE WAS a PA on the coach, and the driver had been playing Christmas songs ever since they had left London: 'Santa Baby,' 'The First Noel,' 'Baby, It's Cold Outside.' It was nice—comfortable—and Milton had even found himself tapping his feet as some of the other passengers joined in. He made his way back up the aisle. Elijah and Sharon were sitting in a pair of seats near the front of the coach, and Milton had a seat to himself on the other side of the aisle. He lowered himself down, moving slowly, wincing as his shoulder touched the back of the seat.

"You okay?" Sharon asked him.

Elijah caught Milton's eye.

"Slept on it," he explained. "Aches and pains. One of the problems about getting old."

"You're not old," Sharon said.

"Yes, he is," Elijah said.

Milton looked across the aisle at the young man, who was smiling ever so slightly.

"This bus probably doesn't help," Sharron said. "The seats aren't the most comfortable."

"You won't be travelling on busses much longer," Milton said.

"We had return tickets," Sharron said. "I didn't bring Elijah up to be wasteful."

Elijah rolled his eyes.

They hadn't told Sharon what had happened in the garage. Milton had left the decision as to what they would say to Elijah, and he had decided that there was no point in worrying her unnecessarily. Milton had imposed what he had thought was right on the young man before, and that hadn't gone so well for him. This time, he had decided that he would step back; Elijah was an adult now, and what happened next was his decision. Milton might not have agreed with his choice—he didn't—but it was his choice to make.

Milton exhaled and looked out of the window. The National Express coach had set off from Victoria coach station at half three, and now, at just before eight, they were approaching Chesterfield.

It had been a long day.

Milton had given thought to whether the police would have been able to put Elijah at the scene of the murders. Ziggy had checked for CCTV at the club and had found nothing to show him and Tiffany Brown leaving together. It did not appear that there were any witnesses who might have seen them, and Elijah had been taken away from the club in the boot of the car. The garages were not overlooked by neighbours, so the events that had taken place inside would not have been noticed, either. The only person who would have been able to put Elijah at the scene of the crime was Tiffany, and she would have had to compromise herself in order to do so. Milton needed to ensure that he was in the clear, too, and had taken the gun with his prints on it and had disposed of it.

Ziggy had found the initial reports that had been filed by the investigating officers who had had their Christmases ruined by the discovery of the four dead men in the Woodford garage, and they had—prompted by the discovery of the cannabis farm—concluded that they had been murdered thanks to a local drug feud.

There was no reference to Tiffany being at the scene; Milton assumed that she had fled. The woman had been interviewed at her home late on Christmas Day and had, according to the reports, been convincing in her grief. No, Tiffany said, she had no idea why her brother was in the garage, and she could not identify the bodies of the three young men who had been found next to him. It didn't take the police long: Solomon Brown, Rowmando Silcott, Tyrone Godwin and Shaquille Abora were confirmed as the dead men, their affiliation with the London Fields Boys was established, and they were marked down as just four more victims of London's postcode war.

Hicks had taken Milton and Elijah back to London. Pinky had taken and destroyed Elijah's phone, so Milton had texted Sharon to say that he was with her son and that the two of them had settled their differences. He told her that Elijah had lost his phone, and that he had asked Milton to tell her that he had gone back to the hotel. Milton didn't say anything else—Sharon would have assumed that her son was with a girl—and she had evidently believed it. Milton didn't like lying to her, but it was what Elijah wanted, and he could see that his motives were pure.

The coach slowed down as they approached the station.

"Another twenty-five minutes and we'll be home," Sharon said. "I hope you're not expecting too much."

"He doesn't care, Mum," Elijah said.

"It's very kind of you to invite me," Milton said.

"What else was I going to do? It's Christmas. You're not spending it on your own."

"It wouldn't have been the first time," Milton said.

"Well, not this year. I've got food in the fridge. You had a Caribbean Christmas dinner before?"

"Never."

"Turkey, ham, pastelles, macaroni pie," she said.

"You got calallo?" Elijah said.

"John won't know what that is."

"Like collard greens," Milton said.

"How'd you know that?"

"I've travelled a bit," Milton said, allowing himself a smile.

"And duchess potatoes, Mum," Elijah said. "Please say you've got duchess potatoes."

"We're not going to eat until midnight if I have to do duchess potatoes."

Milton turned away from the two of them and looked out of the window again. Snow had been falling throughout their journey, with more of it the farther north that they had travelled. The pavements around the coach station had been cleared, but several inches had settled on the cars that had been parked next to the depot. Milton saw his reflection in the glass and closed his eyes. He would have been happy to spend the day in his hotel room, waiting to take the next flight back to Tenerife, but he had wanted to make sure that Elijah and Sharon returned home without any further incident.

That was what he told himself, anyway. Elijah had suggested he spend a couple of days with them, and Sharon had quickly agreed; Milton had not been able to say no.

The brakes wheezed as the driver angled the bus into the bay and disgorged the passengers who were finishing their journeys here. Milton reached into his bag, took out his phone, and slipped his AirPods into his ears. He scrolled through his playlists, found his Bauhaus albums, and hit play. The coach jerked into motion again as the driver backed out of the bay. Milton listened to Peter Murphy's rich baritone and closed his eyes.

JOIN THE READERS' CLUB

Building a relationship with my readers is the very best thing about writing. I occasionally send newsletters with details on new releases, special offers and other bits of news relating to the Milton, Beatrix and Isabella Rose and Soho Noir series.

If you join my Readers' Club I'll send you this free Milton content:

1. A free copy of Milton's adventure in North Korea - '1000 Yards.'

2. A free copy of Milton's tussle with a Mafia assassin in 'Tarantula.'

3. An eyes-only profile of Milton from a Group Fifteen psychologist.

You can get your free content by visiting my website at markjdawson.com. I'll look forward to seeing you there.

ALSO BY MARK DAWSON

IN THE JOHN MILTON SERIES

The Cleaner

Sharon Warriner is a single mother in the East End of London, fearful that she's lost her young son to a life in the gangs. After John Milton saves her life, he promises to help. But the gang, and the charismatic rapper who leads it, is not about to cooperate with him.

Saint Death

John Milton has been off the grid for six months. He surfaces in Ciudad Juárez, Mexico, and immediately finds himself drawn into a vicious battle with the narco-gangs that control the borderlands.

The Driver

When a girl he drives to a party goes missing, John Milton is worried. Especially when two dead bodies are discovered and the police start treating him as their prime suspect.

Buy The Driver

Ghosts

John Milton is blackmailed into finding his predecessor as Number One. But she's a ghost, too, and just as dangerous as him. He finds himself in deep trouble, playing the Russians against the British in a desperate attempt to save the life of his oldest friend.

Buy Ghosts

The Sword of God

On the run from his own demons, John Milton treks through the Michigan wilderness into the town of Truth. He's not looking for trouble, but trouble's looking for him. He finds himself up against a small-town cop who has no idea with whom he is dealing, and no idea how dangerous he is.

Buy The Sword of God

Salvation Row

Milton finds himself in New Orleans, returning a favour that saved his life during Katrina. When a lethal adversary from his past takes an interest in his business, there's going to be hell to pay.

Buy Salvation Row

Headhunters

Milton barely escaped from Avi Bachman with his life. But when the Mossad's most dangerous renegade agent breaks out of a maximum security prison, their second fight will be to the finish.

Buy Headhunters

The Ninth Step

Milton's attempted good deed becomes a quest to unveil corruption at the highest levels of government and murder at the dark heart of the criminal underworld. Milton is pulled back into the game, and that's going to have serious consequences for everyone who crosses his path.

Buy The Ninth Step

The Jungle

John Milton is no stranger to the world's seedy underbelly. But when the former British Secret Service agent comes up against a ruthless human trafficking ring, he'll have to fight harder than ever to conquer the evil in his path.

Buy The Jungle

Blackout

A message from Milton's past leads him to Manila and a

confrontation with an adversary he thought he would never meet again. Milton finds himself accused of murder and imprisoned inside a brutal Filipino jail - can he escape, uncover the truth and gain vengeance for his friend?

Buy Blackout

The Alamo

A young boy witnesses a murder in a New York subway restroom. Milton finds him, and protects him from corrupt cops and the ruthless boss of a local gang.

Buy The Alamo

Redeemer

Milton is in Brazil, helping out an old friend with a close protection business. When a young girl is kidnapped, he finds himself battling a local crime lord to get her back.

Buy Redeemer

Sleepers

When a Russian defector is assassinated in a sleepy English seaside town, Group Fifteen agents John Milton and Michael Pope find themselves in a rush to uncover the culprits and bring them to justice.

Buy Sleepers

IN THE BEATRIX ROSE SERIES

In Cold Blood

Beatrix Rose was the most dangerous assassin in an off-the-books government kill squad until her former boss betrayed her. A decade later, she emerges from the Hong Kong underworld with payback on her mind. They gunned down her husband and kidnapped her daughter, and now the debt needs to be repaid. It's a blood feud she didn't start but she is going to finish.

Blood Moon Rising

There were six names on Beatrix's Death List and now there are four. She's going to account for the others, one by one, even if it kills her. She has returned from Somalia with another target in her sights. Bryan Duffy is in Iraq, surrounded by mercenaries, with no easy way to get to him and no easy way to get out. And Beatrix has other issues that need to be addressed. Will Duffy prove to be one kill too far?

Buy Blood Moon Rising

Blood and Roses

Beatrix Rose has worked her way through her Kill List. Four are dead, just two are left. But now her foes know she has them in her sights and the hunter has become the hunted.

Buy Blood and Roses

Hong Kong Stories, Vol. 1

Beatrix Rose flees to Hong Kong after the murder of her husband and the kidnapping of her child. She needs money. The local triads have it. What could possibly go wrong?

Buy Hong Kong Stories

Phoenix

She does Britain's dirty work, but this time she needs help. Beatrix Rose, meet John Milton...

Buy Phoenix

IN THE ISABELLA ROSE SERIES

The Angel

Isabella Rose is recruited by British intelligence after a terrorist attack on Westminster.

Buy The Angel

The Asset

Isabella Rose, the Angel, is used to surprises, but being abducted is an unwelcome novelty. She's relying on Michael Pope, the head of the top-secret Group Fifteen, to get her back.

Buy The Asset

The Agent

Isabella Rose is on the run, hunted by the very people she had been hired to work for. Trained killer Isabella and former handler Michael Pope are forced into hiding in India and, when a mysterious informer passes them clues on the whereabouts of Pope's family, the prey see an opportunity to become the predators.

Buy The Asset

The Assassin

Ciudad Juárez, Mexico, is the most dangerous city in the world. And when a mission to break the local cartel's grip goes wrong, Isabella Rose, the Angel, finds herself on the wrong side of prison bars. Fearing the worst, Isabella plays her only remaining card...

Buy The Assassin

IN THE SOHO NOIR SERIES

Gaslight

When Harry and his brother Frank are blackmailed into paying off a local hood they decide to take care of the problem themselves. But when all of London's underworld is in thrall to the man's boss, was their plan audacious or the most foolish thing that they could possibly have done?

Free Download

The Black Mile

London, 1940: the Luftwaffe blitzes London every night for fifty-seven nights. Houses, shops and entire streets are wiped from the map. The underworld is in flux: the Italian criminals who dominated the West End have been interned and now their rivals are fighting to replace them. Meanwhile, hidden in the shadows, the Black-Out Ripper sharpens his knife and sets to his grisly work.

Get The Black Mile

The Imposter

War hero Edward Fabian finds himself drawn into a criminal family's web of vice and soon he is an accomplice to their scheming. But he's not the man they think he is - he's far more dangerous than they could possibly imagine.

Get The Imposter

ABOUT THE AUTHOR

Mark Dawson is the author of the breakout John Milton, Beatrix and Isabella Rose and Soho Noir series.

For more information:
www.markjdawson.com
mark@markjdawson.com

AN UNPUTDOWNABLE ebook.
First published in Great Britain in 2013 by UNPUTDOWNABLE LIMITED
Ebook first published in 2013 by UNPUTDOWNABLE LIMITED

❀ Created with Vellum